Zindel   c.1
When a darkness falls.

32

13.95

WHEN A DARKNESS FALLS

MAR 2 2 1984

WHEN A DARKNESS FALLS

PAUL ZINDEL

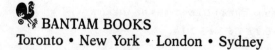

BANTAM BOOKS
Toronto • New York • London • Sydney

WHEN A DARKNESS FALLS
A Bantam Book / March 1984

Library of Congress Cataloging in Publication Data

Zindel, Paul.
  When a darkness falls.

  I. Title.
PS3576.I518W5 1984   813'.54   83-21392
ISBN 0-553-05030-3

Published simultaneously in the United States and Canada

Bantam Books are published by Bantam Books, Inc. Its trade-
mark, consisting of the words "Bantam Books" and the por-
trayal of a rooster, is Registered in the United States Patent and
Trademark Office and in other countries. Marca Registrada. Ban-
tam Books, Inc., 666 Fifth Avenue, New York, New York 10103.

PRINTED IN THE UNITED STATES OF AMERICA

FG   0 9 8 7 6 5 4 3 2 1

WHEN A
DARKNESS
FALLS

PROLOGUE

SPRING, 1981

Lichteiman had been driving, his stomach groaning from a tremendous breakfast of silver-dollar pancakes with a side of Spencer steak, when the report came in over the radio telling him the new nightmare was beginning. Minutes later he turned into a tree-lined parking lot and halted behind the crowd of police and other emergency vehicles. He climbed out, opened his belt and the top of his pants to let his white Mexican shirt spill over and down to disguise his swollen belly. As he walked across the lawn he wondered how the young teachers who had graduated from their UCLA education courses straight into this horror, would explain what had happened: *"Now, children, we're very sorry but last night some very bad, bad person broke into our school and did things, he did very bad things . . ."*

The teachers had gathered the children in the picnic area of the park and parents were already beginning to arrive to take them home. The children were having their milk snack and riding the swings and seesaws, but every few moments they would look across the playing field to their nursery school building and the barricades surrounding the park bathrooms nearby. As Lichteiman passed the kids he found himself trying to slip into their brains, trying to see the event through their eyes.

"Did they do it to our rabbit?" a little boy in designer jeans wanted to know.

"Yep," another boy answered. "They did it to the rabbit and the chicken and the parakeet, too . . ."

One of the other children began to tremble, then burst into tears. "Everything's going to be fine," a teacher said soothingly as she passed out raisins. "Your mommies and daddies are coming to get you . . ."

Lichteiman stopped at the school building first. Inside the adobe and stucco walls he was acknowledged, but stayed apart from the other detectives and a couple of park attendants who were already doing the cleanup.

"The main event's in the lavatory," Gower, one of the newer detectives, told him.

One of the teachers was lifting a limp furry form from a closet gently, as though it were a child. She was crying, bewildered, and one of the cops tried to comfort her.

Tolman came over. "School started at eight forty-five. They knew the animals were missing and then some kid found them in the closet. We didn't find the body out *there* until ten, fifteen minutes ago."

Lichteiman looked out through the window, through the translucent owls and flowers the children had painted on the glass. Tolman went on: "They cut the heads off the animals with a pair of scissors. Imagine, cutting heads off little animals. A couple of parakeets, a white hen. Ya know how much strength it takes to scissor the head off an Australian jackrabbit?"

One of the teachers offered Lichteiman a container of milk. He took it, opened its spout and put a straw inside. Sipping, he felt its coldness rushing down, soothing his throbbing stomach.

"Thank you," he finally muttered, and began to move about the classroom. The walls were covered with the kids' art work. Crayon drawings of airplanes, watercolor rainbows. One shelf was a line of small old lady dolls with dried apples for heads. Through the window he could see the lightning from flashbulbs reflecting off the brick entrance walls of the smaller lavatory building beyond. The coroner and assistant were arriving. He'd give them a few minutes before moving in, as Tolman said, on the "main event." For the moment he let his eyes drift over the penmanship charts and the block pile and the cubbyholes labeled Jimmy W. and Sandra and Tommy and Jason and Jimmy K. and . . . in the middle of the fingerpaints and the midget chairs and the *I Can Read* books and the scattered volumes of Maurice Sendaks and Dr. Seuss, was the black plastic bag which would be collected by the special refuse truck. It wasn't the first time a school had had its pet animals mutilated, Lichteiman recalled. Older kids sometimes remember things they hated about nursery school, like the teacher who made them eat rice pudding or stand in a corner. Then one night they get high and decide to cause a little misery. Most times, fingerprintings no good 'cause the punks don't have fingerprint records yet. And they usually don't do it twice.

Lichteiman moved slowly outside, began walking the few hundred feet along the school grounds, to the smaller brick building in the park. On his left was a wood-slat fence through which he could see the school's yard, littered with tricycles and wagons, with a pole horse suspended on a thick metal spring. Not far off, near the street, were two public phones, benches, and a grape arbor. A Theta Cable truck, a telephone truck, and two other vans stood at the curb. Cops were questioning the workmen who stopped for a peaceful coffee break, a sandwich, a place to rest or call their lover or wife, or read a magazine, even masturbate.

He paused. It was in the faces of the cops manning the barricades as they grimly nodded hello. They knew him, he was the specialist, and as they moved a wooden horse to allow him access, Lichteiman felt them keep their distance. They were surprised to see him detour to the right and enter the men's room. Inside it was pleasantly cool and, he noticed, free of graffiti. He relieved himself.

Outside again, he moved to the other entrance. The police photographer was still shooting, a fingerprint squad was at work—the coroner, Doc Heybrown, who always wore a blue pinstripe suit with a loud, clashing tie, came up from a squat into Lichteiman's view.

"Who is she?" Lichteiman asked.

"Don't know, probably a whore—but she didn't deserve this," Doc said.

There, on the cold Mexican tile floor lay the girl. She was tied—with her hands high over her head, so that she appeared to have been praying when death came.

Now, here, an unnamed presentiment took hold, tightening Lichteiman's chest. When he moved closer, around the body, he wasn't quite prepared for the sight of the silver, shiny loops of a scissors' handle protruding from her neck. The weapon had been thrust into the skin just below her left ear. It looked like a monstrous piece of jewelry.

A couple of the other detectives started filling him in, their low voices echoing like mourning chants in the tiled chamber. "We figure none of the teachers came in here this morning. Even if they missed the body they would have seen the scratching on the walls and the kicked and dented metal."

Lichteiman listened, but his eyes were on a large smashed mirror above the sink. The mirror reflected a ruptured image back at him, a bursting fiend of cracked silvered glass. Then the odor reached his nostrils and he began to choke.

"Whoever did it killed her, then pissed on her," one of the detectives whispered.

Lichteiman hastened outside, stopping only when he had reached the heat of the sun. The shadows, and the blurred phantom of a wild animal barking, prowled at the fringe of his reason. *Take a little girl through your window, take a little girl through your window*—the children were singing across the park.

He would go home, wait a week, a month—sometimes it had been longer. A coldness deep inside his brain told him it was just a matter of time. Soon his special talent would be needed.

PART I

CHAPTER ONE

JULY 8
MIDNIGHT

Now there were sounds. Sounds.

She hadn't gotten used to the sounds of the home—the creakings, expansions, the *settlings*, as the geologist had called them. "Yes, the east portion of the home is settling. You can tell by the cracks near the fireplace. And there are termites, but we'll wrap the house. We'll put a great plastic wrapping around the house and pour in the lethal gas until the termites retreat deep into the ground to hide with the termite queen, two hundred, three hundred feet below. And then the little devils can start crawling up again, and in a few years we'll just wrap and gas again."

Marjorie was writing her novel late in the guest room. She tried to keep all the rules of storytelling in her head. She needed to maintain the energy, the tension. If she could only hold onto the vision of one young person to tell her entire story to, but it had been eight years since she had left high school teaching, and its madness of staff meetings, lesson plans and quick, quick youth. Now the only teenager she'd spoken to for more than a moment had been some stoned star's son who showed up to cut down a diseased eucalyptus tree in the backyard. In New York the young had sort of shouted and poured over her in the classrooms and streets. But here in Beverly Hills, youth kept its drugged distance. Bleached, laid back, on the beach or occasionally screaming at her from Lamborghinis or Trans Ams cruising Sunset.

Sounds again.

She got up from her white wicker desk to check out a front window. Usually, there was at least one coyote out near the street light waiting for garbage night, Thursday, when it would go to work and tear at the plastic bags of refuse and custom outsized green garbage cans that squatted outside of the huge houses on the street.

Nothing.

Her eyes checked the shadows of ivy for rats, cats. Perhaps a rattlesnake; she knew when the full summer heat hit the canyons at the dead end of the street these thermostatless creatures advanced toward the coolness of the green lawns and pools. Mr. Mercer, a neighbor, had told her he'd found three last summer, had chopped their heads off with a shovel. But then again Mercer seemed the kind of neighbor who would always be hunting something—gophers, night crawlers, *jokes*. Every utterance from him seemed to be a nervous search for a joke!

Click!

Clunk!

She moved out of the guest room, into the hall. From her workroom it was like looking down a short city block to the master suite. Through a glass wall she saw the backyard: the rabbits, safe and white— they had bought them in Tahoe for the children's Easter. No raccoons trying to split their metal cage apart. No dogs barking. No toads, snakes, or rats struggling in the pool. The night lights illuminated just enough to see the eucalyptus giants, still erect, not about to smash into the children's bedrooms.

Crunch! Click!

Next she'd check Courtney's room, down the hallway before the great spiral entrance which welded the bottom half of the house to the top. Her beloved Courtney with a touch of asthma—the treasure who woke up at all hours, who would sometimes rush down to leap into their bed and then have to be moved to the special foam couch they kept on hand, ready for frightened, thirsty, love-needing children in the night.

Courtney was asleep in her double-decker FAO Schwartz dollhouse bed, sprawled out voluptuously and tall, all ninety-seven-percentile length of her. She was a princess skyjumper, falling against the white clouds of sheeting and dolls and an acre of lace-trimmed comforter. One of the sliding windows toward the front of the house was open. The curtain moved, sent slow breaths of air toward her daughter. She locked the window; it was too near the main entrance. Someone could climb over the wrought-iron ornamental guard rails and harm her little wild girl. She marveled at her perfection, covered her, and headed back out the door. She paused a moment—started back as she often did—to gasp at the collection of dolls, stereo, bulletin board, posters, and closet bursting with clothes. She felt an assault of extra love for her husband for letting her so indulge her children.

Back down the hall now past her office, down the three steps to the L-turn. There was the short side hall, then Danny's room, vast and red, an artist's loft. Her six-year-old son lay half hanging out of his car bed, his neck limp, his beautiful brown hair fallen downward. Ouch! She stepped on one of the midget race cars, tiptoed over the dominoes and silent battery toys. She strained turning him, lifting him, resetting his head on the center of the Superman pillow. She kissed him, moved his Binky and Paddington Bear and the stuffed camel so they surrounded him, protected him. The writer part of her brain began to hum: *And when they write your history, my sweet son, yours will not be the saga of a family in crisis, nor the marital discord of Adam and Eve. Your odyssey will occur together with your sister and your loving mother and father, most of it preserved on home movies and VHS tape cassettes played on our Panasonic TV. We were a family essential and valiant and in love . . .*

Back in her office she began to jot down these night thoughts for her novel. Keep it from the gut, she kept telling herself. From the gut. Her fear. State her fear. There *are* shadows out there, building, forming to tear apart other families.

Clunk.

The *sounds* again. They came from below. She didn't like to go down the servant stairs, but that's where the noise was. *In the kitchen.* She turned left in the hall, down past the service entrance and garage. She checked the locks, continued downward. *Bitch!* Her robe caught on a banister. Then her bare feet hit the cheap linoleum tile. Yes, *the kitchen.* Someone had been there. She had interrupted something. Maybe Maria guzzling the grape juice, eating sugar wafers or Wheat Thins, raiding the freezer in the laundry room.

She flicked on the lights.

No one.

The door to the maid's bedroom was closed. Now *breathing,* the rattle of metal. Her ears knew that sound—Sandy, the Airedalesque mutt she'd saved from the pound's decompression chamber that would have slaughtered the animal by making it explode from within. Sandy, contained in the alcove between the maid's bath and the far door to the backyard.

Now at last a clue: a milk container left on the white tile of the oven island. That would be Jack: her husband who liked a glass of milk in the middle of the night. She checked the munchies cabinet. Everything still neat. Sunflower seeds and almonds for her, Triscuits, Baby Ruths, pretzels and salted pumpkin seeds for Jack. The vast cache of sugar donuts, Zingers, candy corn, and fortune cookies for the kids.

Just the milk.

She was surprised he'd left it out; thankful she'd come along to save it. She opened the refrigerator and was about to replace it on the top shelf, when something made her smell it. It nearly passed her nose test, but not quite. She checked the date. It should still be good, but it *wasn't*. The milk was cold, but *foul*. She poured it down the drain.

Jack was asleep by the time she'd made it upstairs. She could never negotiate that stretch behind the slab of hallway windows on either floor without feeling like a plastic bear in a shooting gallery. Every few steps she imagined a bullet from a light gun would strike a photo-electric cell in her shoulder and she'd growl, throw up her arms, and keel over. There would be drapes when they could afford them.

She climbed in on the left side, *her* side of the bed. Carefully. Not *too* carefully. This might be one of the many evenings her sweet and tired husband would stir, find himself erect, and move upon her like a loving incubus. Recently their days had been so exhausting their lovemaking seemed to occur during the late night or in the dawn. Sometimes, when the maid was off on Sunday or Monday, and when the children were at a play date or camp, there would be daylight coupling in the pool or even in the hammock near the rose garden.

Not tonight. Instead she decided to construct her

dreams. She let her leg touch his, soon she found herself floating back into a night memory. She was pushing the double walker in Central Park when the children were two and four, with the heat muffling the traffic noises on the parkway and the cries of blacks on skateboards. The joy of horses pulling the ornate horse-drawn carriages. Kids screaming from swings. Old friends and English nannies. The Ethical Culture School. Sipping coffee with the other mothers. Shortbread recipes. New School bulletins. In the night's eye she saw Courtney with a pull toy, and Danny with his roaring tank. And now Jack was hurrying up from the path by the Tavern on the Green. A script meeting at ABC or NBC. And then, the hugs and kisses of their park reunion. *Daddy, Daddy, let me show you this; Daddy, put me on your shoulders. I love you Daddy . . .*

JULY 21

Marjorie was the first one awake on this morning of their anniversary. She put on her robe, closed the door to her husband's separate sink and dressing area. The endless doors—the sliding kind that came out of the wall—were still strange to her. Feeble little brass-plated locks that didn't really work. She moved through her excessively large marble bathroom straight out into the hallway, then circled back to close the second entrance of the bedroom to protect Jack's sleep. Attached to the door handle was the long leash, and at the end of it, Sam.

Sam moaned, staggered to his feet. Marjorie rushed him downstairs to Sandy's sleeping alcove and let them both outside. The technique of mildly restraining the Great Dane in the upper hallway was the only way to protect the house from being devoured while they slept. Sam's black hugeness gave her a tremendous sense of safety. From Sam's sleeping space he could see if anyone entered, anyone evil, intent on hurting her or Jack or the children at the far end. If an intruder came, there would be that transition from Sam, dumb, happy, and foolish to Sam, black and gnashing, a loyal killing machine, quite capable of tearing the thin leather leash from the knob.

By 8:10, the morning chaos.

"Mommy, there's a girl in my class who says her dress had another person in it," Court said, slapping her dish of AlphaBits, then knocking a glass of orange juice onto the already distressed wood of the table. Maria had burned the coffee. The gardener, Tomás, had arrived, made his rounds of the backyard, and was already deep into brushing the tile of the pool as if removing a ring from a very large bathtub.

"Did you brush your teeth, Danny?"

Jack came down in his Superdad nightshirt, barefoot, still waking up. The kiss for Marjorie, then Danny and a peck for Court.

"Hurry, the camp van is here." The dash for the knapsacks. The last minute art show. "I made a watermelon out of a piece of wood, Daddy." "Daddy, buy me an E.T. toothbrush." "I love you, Daddy."

"Win a lot of ribbons," Jack called after them. Marjorie rushed them through the kitchen, up the steps and out the service door. The sight of the camp bus with the giant letters "Camp Kushaqua" was still a little more than she could bear, considering the price of the tuition, but it was the day camp where all the kids from school were going; an acre near the veterans' hospital and graveyard, of all places.

"Drive carefully, Joey," Marjorie only half-kidded with the young driver.

"You bet, Mrs. Krenner. The kids are going to cut a trail today."

"That's wonderful," Marjorie agreed—then had a vision of toddlers at hard labor, swinging scythes.

The van drove off and Marjorie rushed back to the breakfast table. A second cup of coffee with her lover and husband. She slipped a small silver-wrapped box from her robe pocket and put it in front of him.

"Happy anniversary," she said.

Jack looked at the present.

"Thanks, Marjorie." He leaned over to kiss her but his lips barely grazed her cheek. She could tell he was embarrassed by the ritual; he had never received a gift gracefully. She also knew he wouldn't open it until he was alone, but then he would see the cufflinks set with the mineral opals she had bought on their March trip to Australia—well, then he would wear them proudly and remember the kangaroos and Great Barrier Reef and duckbilled platypi . . .

"Look, Marjorie, I've been a little freaked out. I've got to have a second draft for Aris by Friday. I'm getting into overload. I didn't get you anything."

"Don't worry about it, Jack. I understand."

"Go down to Rodeo Drive and pick yourself out something. I was going to get you another Last Chance day at Elizabeth Arden but I forgot. I feel dead."

"You look good to me," Marjorie winked, and got a smile out of him. And she meant it. She had always found him entirely handsome, had always wanted to be so close to him that she might pour into his skin and become one with him. She adored him even on the few occasions she believed he was entirely exhausted, because weariness only made his dark eyes slow and his full lips all the more magnetic. He had lips like her father had when he was alive, and the same rich dark hair which broke in the middle.

"By the way, you left the milk out last night," Marjorie said.

"No, I didn't. I don't think so."

"Well, somebody did," she smiled. "Want some more coffee?"

She cherished the minutes before he would stand up, leave the breakfast table, and walk the length of the lower floor to his library-office. Now with the children gone, the servants busy, he would sip his second cup of coffee and give her the benefit of his wisdom. She felt linked to him, as if only through him could she ever really become who she was meant to be. And yet, she felt this gift was no more than she had given him. In her insistence that she be an equal contributor to their marriage they both knew she had given him his fullest sexuality.

"Jack, about the young girl in my novel," she began shyly. "You know, my girl who is unable to admit that her father is dead? Do you remember, in my book?"

"Yes, I remember."

"I thought perhaps I'd do better making her conflict arise out of her exposure to the boy's crazed world. Do you think that would work? Do you think that could be the trigger?"

Jack oracled a response about the importance of Marjorie deciding what problem she wanted to solve before assigning the task to any of her characters—then disappeared for his own work in his library.

In less than an hour the call came in from New York and she had to tell him his mother was dying.

CHAPTER TWO

JULY 22
4:30 A.M.

At first, when the phone rang so early, Lichteiman thought it would be his old friend Harry—but before he lifted the receiver to his ear he knew it couldn't be Harry Duckman because Harry was in Hawaii for the rest of his life with a gold watch or whatever the boys had decided to buy him.

"What?" he shouted into the phone.

"George Lichteiman?"

"You got him."

"This is Lieutenant Straub. I've taken over Lieutenant Duckman's job."

"What do you want?" Lichteiman wheezed. He was sitting on the edge of his bed, looking down at his huge thighs thrusting out from under his nightshirt. Two hundred and eighty pounds. He'd need more than Pritikin. Was there really no going back? Fifty-seven years old with the big six-o creeping up and this obtrusive voice in his ear at this hour of the morning. A new lieutenant could be a pain in the ass, but Lichteiman heard respect in the voice. That meant someone had already told Straub about him—about Lichteiman the volatile, half-cocked madman, the impulsive wiseass reactionary who had called the Police Commissioner an "asshole" in front of eight hundred rich matrons at a political dinner. *Oh, yeah, you gotta call Lichteiman in on this one. Fat old Lichteiman who lives up on Mulholland Drive in the ugly old house straddling the mountain top.* Good old Lichteiman, tough, loud mouth, good at boozing, brawling, and gambling. *Oh, you really heard things about me, Eddie Straub, I can tell. The time I got stabbed in the heart in San Francisco and rumors that I broke seventeen bones on a pimp and threw a pusher off the roof. Yeah, yeah, the whole story . . .*

"It's your kind," Eddie Straub told him.

Lichteiman hung up without a response. Feet into boots, no time for socks, no underpants, need trousers, tuck the nightshirt in. Can't let the mind start working yet. If the mind started, he'd be an hour late. Back to the bedstand; cash, a few coins, and the safari jacket to cover a multitude of sins.

Outside, his eyes began to water. He felt pains in his chest, the kind he used to think meant heart attack or advanced emphysema. Long ago he had learned they were only the signal of a second-stage smog alert. He got into his brown '73 Fleetwood, turned the key. The engine coughed with resentment. He rolled down the long dirt driveway, and turned right. Taking one hand off the steering wheel, he pressed the catch of the glove compartment, and grabbed a pint bottle of Jack Daniels.

Eddie Straub looked even more like a wimp than Lichteiman had imagined, young, handsome, sandy hair, a mouth-breather. Straub was waiting by the body, which had been discovered in a rubbish heap next to a soccer field. Four squad cars were parked on the field, their roof lights flashing in the dawn. The Investigative Service van backed up closer to the covered body, which lay near a soiled mattress.

Straub introduced himself, spoke quickly. "Some

millionaire soap manufacturer found the body when
he was walking his dog. The victim is female, around
twenty, could have been a hitchhiker—hippie-type."

"Don't like hippies, Straub?" Lichteiman asked.

Straub paused, then decided to ignore the question. "She's been dead nine days. Stabbed thirty-seven
times with something like an ice pick."

"You said it was *my* kind?" Lichteiman said
slowly.

"She was under the mattress. Kids use this field
every day for soccer practice, dozens of kids. The guy
had the dog on a leash and he saw her left arm stick-
ing out from under."

"So what?"

"That body's been under that mattress for nine
days, but somebody moved the *arm* out last night. If it
had been out before that, kids would have seen it."

Lichteiman frowned, irritated that his morning
sleep could be at the mercy of this newcomer. He
scanned the technicians crouching to peel dried blood
from clothing and clay. They were going over the mattress with a fine-tooth comb. Straub was technically
fine, Lichteiman thought, but he would be missing
that special sixth sense. Lichteiman fought down the
urge to start roaring at him. *So, what does it mean? A
couple of kids were playing on the mattress yesterday.
They lifted it up and saw a corpse, screamed, dropped
the mattress down and the arm was flung out and exposed. Check around. A frightened kid somewhere would
have to tell somebody. That's how the arm got out, you
overpaid bozo . . .*

"Some children may have disturbed the body,"
Lichteiman said with control.

"There's *more* than the hand," Eddie Straub said.

Straub pulled back the grey canvas cover, exposing the young, lifeless form. The girl's body was un-

clothed. Most of the punctures were in the lower abdominal region. Lichteiman's eyes moved from the dried, near-black wounds up to what he could only imagine had once been a pretty, young face. It *was* his kind of case, he knew, even before Straub told him why.

"The thing is," Straub now stressed, "she died nine days ago from twenty-eight of the stab wounds, but *nine of the wounds are newer*. Whoever it was came back, *stabbed the dead body again—stabbed the body more than a week after it was dead!*"

Lichteiman wheeled around and plodded toward his car. Straub shouted after him.

"Your kind, Lichteiman! Was I right?"

Lichteiman remembered the body crumpled in the park bathroom, a corpse rank with urine.

Something insane was loose in the world. Again.

You were right, Straub.

JULY 23

It was decided at dinner that Jack had to make the trip East alone. Jack said there was not enough money for them all to go, and besides Marjorie had never been close to his mother or sister. She had always considered them rather eccentric, dominating characters whose lifetime of struggle to survive Jack's mother's early divorce had left deep, painful scars. Marjorie also felt herself somehow the subject of ridicule in their eyes, almost as though Jack had tricked her into marriage, and she hated their constant portrayal of Jack as some sort of *enfant terrible* whose artistic temperament deserved total support, especially from his cretin Jewish wife.

Marjorie drove Jack to the airport that night for a redeye special, and they made the decision to tell the kids that Grandma Mary was dying. When she got back that evening, Marjorie pulled a few books from the library, ones she had bought when her own father had died three years earlier, but the children didn't ask the questions she knew they would ask now. She had *About Dying*, and *The 10th Good Thing About Barney*, and *My Grandpa Died Today*.

She was fairly well prepared by the time the kids got home from camp the next day. She cooked their favorite breaded veal for dinner, with steamed carrots for Courtney and raw carrots for Danny. She let them make chocolate chip ice cream sundaes for dessert, topped with sprinkles and Magic Shell. Just before *The Muppets* Courtney asked what being dead *meant*.

"Have you ever seen anything dead?" Marjorie asked.

"Dead *grass*," Danny blurted, and laughed.

"Dead is when you don't move," Courtney said. "I saw a dead mouse and a dead goldfish and a dead fly."

"Dead is when Daddy yells at you and you say you wish you were dead, right Mommy?"

Marjorie was startled by Danny's question. She didn't remember saying any such thing. "*No*. If I ever said that I didn't mean it, and I apologize to you both. It was a silly thing for me to say." She had forgotten how literally kids take phrases like "You're killing me," or "Oh, yes, please, I'm dying to go." She must remember to ask the kids to tell her at the end of the discussion exactly what, in their own words, did they think they had been told. "Do I often mention dying after a fight with your Daddy?" she asked.

"That's bad stuff," Courtney said. "Let's not talk about *bad stuff*."

"That's okay. I think we should talk about it, if you want to."

Marjorie could see both Danny and Courtney

were beginning to look uncomfortable. "Do you remember *when* I said I wished I was dead?"

"It was the time, one time when this man came over and gave you a hug, he put his hand around your shoulder . . . and Daddy said . . ."

"What did Daddy say, Courtney?"

"Daddy started yelling," Danny laughed.

"And *why* did Daddy start yelling?"

"Because that man called the house the next morning and Daddy got woked up, and the man said he was calling because his daughter's birthday party was going to be at the Santa Monica Playhouse on Fourth Street and the invitation said Eighth Street—and Daddy started yelling and yelling.

"I don't want my birthday party at the Santa Monica Playhouse . . ."

Marjorie was astounded to hear the kids had remembered what was really a very innocent incident. One of the fathers had greeted her with a hug at a parents' night in a crowd of four hundred people. The guy had had a couple of drinks, but he had known her and Jack from the kids' soccer league; he had a lovely daughter, Holly, and a pleasant, silly-looking wife, and Jack had blown the whole thing out of proportion with his explosive jealousy. The whole incident had been just one more slap against her, and she was tired of the campaign Jack had been waging to totally control her every move. There had been three entire months with him interrogating her about where she had been, whom she had seen, what had taken so long going from Gelson's Market to Toys "R" Us. She had finally been asked to account for every half hour, and that was when she exploded right back at Jack and told him to *lay off,* and yes, she probably had dramatically said she wished she was dead. But she hadn't been serious.

"God protects us from death," Danny blurted.

"Oh, yes. He's very nice," Courtney insisted, with a giggle.

Marjorie and Danny had to laugh too. Courtney was always the flirt and entertainer.

"And if I ever met God," Courtney went on, "I'd like to say thank you for the land, thank you for California, thank you for Cal-ifor*nayeaaaah*, New York, Africa, and thank you Johnny Appleseed for the trees.

"Do *you* want to thank God for anything?" Courtney asked Danny.

"Oh yes, I want to thank him for farts . . ."
Danny and Courtney screamed with delight.

Marjorie made a scolding face that made Danny and Courtney howl even more.

"And God's a man who's in a stick, a bone, and rocks and clouds!" Courtney went on.

"And He's in Miss Maggie naked . . ."

"Watch your mouth, Danny."

"And He's in peanut butter," Courtney added. "God's in shadows and trees . . ."

"He's a little man who lives in tiny places, in airports, and in little tiny brains . . ."

"And He's in mouses . . ."

"And He does *this*!" Danny said moving his right hand up and down, then across his chest.

Marjorie was aghast at the sight of Danny crossing himself. She and Jack had never even mentioned religion to the kids. They had been waiting, for *what* she wasn't quite sure. How two agnostics were to educate their kids about religion was one number she hadn't had the faintest idea about. But now, making the sign of the cross . . .

"Do you know what you've just done?" Marjorie asked Danny.

"It's a sign."

"What kind of sign do you think it is?"

"It's a *Jewish*."

"A *Jewish*?"

"Yes. A Jewish or a Catholic sign for children to bless themselves."

"What's a blessing?" Courtney demanded to know.

"I don't know," Danny confessed. "Something to do with vampires. And they do it at accidents or when people hurt other people. And they do it when Mommies and Daddies hurt children and children are put in wooden boxes and put in the ground . . ."

Marjorie sipped a cup of coffee, tried to be natural, remove her emotion. They were both watching her now, hanging on her every move, her every breath. *They were testing.* "Where did you see children in wooden boxes?" she asked.

"On the *news*," Danny said. "We see them on the *news*."

"Like in the war?"

"Yes, the dead kids in the war and the place where all the Spanish gangs and drug addicts shoot each other," Danny explained.

"And sometimes a Mommy throws her kids off a bridge, and we saw a Daddy who shot *everybody*. A little girl and a little boy and they were in the wooden boxes . . ."

"Is that what they're going to do with Grandma? Stick her in a box and plant her?"

Marjorie could feel their anxiety, the nervous wonder and apprehension building in the children now. The joking and fooling around were giving way to something else now, and she knew from the books that children *do* feel very deep emotions about death, that to *avoid* giving them words for the experience could not only be confusing but the source of extreme misconceptions. Something new to worry about. Like Courtney's recent asthmatic episodes. Granted, the attacks were mild, usually following a cold—but they were serious enough to require treatment with Theodar and Alupont. The doctors told her Courtney's asthma was very common in second born children, that often the pressure of keeping up with an older sibling combined with the fact that the parents are often less sensitive the second time around could produce these symptoms.

Just as Marjorie prepared to launch into a description of a funeral ceremony, both children turned away.

The Muppets. Here come the goddamn Muppets.

Marjorie looked at the smiling faces of Courtney and Danny, squealing, turning up the TV volume as they finished off their sundaes. She thought how terribly clever it was of nature to give children such a short sadness span.

JULY 24

It was already rush hour by the time Jack landed at Kennedy. He got his bags, picked up his rental car from Hertz, and moved in the bumper-to-bumper traffic along the expressway. On the Verrazano Bridge, he was overcome with memories. Without a father, the terrain of his childhood had been rough going. From the high point of the bridge, he could only remember the pain. The time in P.S. 26 when someone cracked him in the head with a ball paddle. A gang calling him names, and him reaching into a shoe box to pull out a torpedo firecracker, sending it through the air to explode on one boy's back. Shame on this childhood, he thought. Shame on all the small neurotic writhings of this impoverished Irish and Italian landscape from which he had escaped. He got off at the Todt Hill Road exit; from the moment his mother had moved there years before, the irony of the name had tugged at his mind: *Death Hill Road*. He parked in front of his mother's small tract house with the white fence and broken-down Karmann Ghia in the driveway. His sister Bernice was at the front door, waving. She came out to intercept him on the porch. Now the embrace. Then she blurted the words.

"Cancer, Jack. They found cancer even in her lung fluid."

His sister fled to the side of the porch, crying, above a lily garden. He let her get herself together, then went in. His mother lay exhausted on a rented hospital bed in the living room facing a long mahogany stereo. The smell of cat urine hit his nostrils. She reached out, wheezed his name. He went, sat beside her, hugged her. A great frailness beneath the girdles of fat that still clung to her lower body. Her face was gaunt. Her eyes wide. Her skull emerged through the wrinkled skin that had once been a fine sweet face.

"How's Danny? Courtney?"

"Great, Mom. How are you?"

"They're coming to stick a needle in me again. I keep filling up with fluid."

She didn't know about the cancer.

Later, a friend, Anna Testa, stayed with her while Jack and his sister went out for dinner and a meeting. There were things to talk about, decisions to be made. In the diner they screamed at each other. Bernice said they shouldn't tell her she had cancer, that she only had *days* to live. Jack yelled back, "Give her a chance. Maybe there's *some* way, some new *cure*. She has the right to know so she can do everything possible!"

"Her body is infested," Bernice said. "Her lungs are being devoured . . ."

"She should be in Memorial. The best hospital . . ."

"Great. Stick her on a private jet and check her into the Beverly Wilshire while you're at it. You're not listening. She has at the most a week. A *week*, Jack!"

In the end he calmed down. With the kind of expenses he was socked into he knew he'd take the path of least resistance. No, his mother wouldn't want any doctors touching her. None of those men handling her. She'd gotten rid of the one man in her life many years before, and decided her body was off limits to the masculine segment of the human race. She had done her best to cripple her daughter as well, he remembered. "Men will be trying to touch you, get you into cars, Bernice—and then do filthy things to you. Men will want to hurt you, Bernice . . ."

The next day his mother wanted a small battery-driven, white plastic fan to help her breathe while she recovered from what she agreed to pretend was pneumonia. Second on her list was a request for an order of shrimp in lobster sauce, which she couldn't eat. Third, she wanted Jack to weed her lily garden. By the afternoon the steel oxygen tank stood next to her bed and plastic tubing snaked from its dials to her nostrils.

AUGUST 5

James Ewing Hospital, First Avenue, Manhattan.
The fifth floor. His mother in the *dying* dormitory, one of a row of seven poor, fading ladies. Between X-

rays and giant shots of chemicals and pills and her hands puffing up because an intravenous had slipped to subcutaneous . . . his mother spoke of nothing but her father. *You would have loved him, Jack. When he died my life went with him. He was the only decent man I ever knew, my father. My father had the fruit truck in Stapleton and we'd go out selling fruit all over the streets. And he made sure I had a tablespoon of fresh orange juice every morning. We would sit on top of the hot air vent in the hallway and make paper planes and they would fly up in the draft. And he'd make us waffles and cinnamon toast, and he'd take naps on the old sofa. And once he took me to South Beach and we went on the ferris wheel and rolled the balls and he won me a snake made of rainbow yarn . . .*

Jack sat to the left of her bed, listening to her gasping words. And Mama, he thought, aren't we going to remember the other things?

The most vivid memory in Jack's life was a terrible cliché. It was too crazy and too common, and he had tired of looking to his childhood to understand his life.

He had been pissing in a doll. Three years old, and Bernice was six years old and she was showing off her little dollie that wet. See, you put the water in her mouth and squeeze her tummy and she makes pishhhy out her hole. And it had actually been his sister who asked him what would happen if he put his penis to the doll's vagina and made water—would the water go up through the doll and come out of the doll's mouth?

Let's try it, Jackie.

Let's try it . . .

Let's . . .

Jack was quite willing to go along with what sounded like a reasonable experiment, when his mother came into the room and began all that terrible screaming. He couldn't understand it, *why, Mommie why are you yelling and grabbing my arm and pulling me you're making me cry Mommie don't drag me across the floor where are you taking me Mommie . . .*

She had dragged him across the kitchen floor to the oven. She turned the oven on, lit a match and came at him and now the scream was clear *I'm going to burn it off, I'm going to burn it . . .*

Jack had to laugh silently at the memory. Here he was, watching his mother die, and listening to her talk about her Poppa and the produce truck, the little stable behind the Grove Street house where he kept a horse—and all the while this casebook boredom was churning in his memory. *I'm going to burn it, we'll burn your dirty thing off . . .*

Of course, she didn't *literally* burn him.

That event was boring, preposterous, a mother's deed from another time, he knew. Now a kid could dance around a maypole waving his penis or stick it into a Ding Dong and a mother wouldn't care. He had been threatened with castration by fire for an act that nowadays would barely gain maternal notice. And he wasn't the only one who had been screwed up as a kid. Marjorie had gotten them into several parenting groups and a lot of the fathers remembered their mothers' overblown reactions to early sex play. He'd never met another man who had a mother that threatened what Mrs. Mary Krenner did, but there were some doozies. And there had been some special circumstances as to why his mother had freaked out. At the end of her third year of marriage Dr. Scala their family physician had called her to tell her that her husband had syphillis and that she shouldn't let him touch her for three weeks. *Ah, let me tell you I learned nobody was going to be taking care of us, Jack. I got your father out of that family bakery with his mother making him stir those big vats and cut out those rolls, and I made him into a cop. I made him take those police tests, I gave him children and he came home to me with syphillis . . . and I'm going to burn your thing off, burn it, burn it . . .*

CHAPTER THREE

AUGUST 7
10 A.M.

Sunshine. Not a cloud in the sky.

God, how it depressed Lichteiman to drive down from his sanctuary. He had the choice of turning left from his driveway onto Mulholland and negotiating those curves on Benedict or turning right and taking Coldwater. Either journey to headquarters was marked with memories of madness. On Benedict he had to pass the spot where the Tate woman had been trussed and hung from the rafters, her stomach split wide to reveal entrails and embryo. On Coldwater he had to pass the site of the Heather case. They had called him in on that one. Blood oozing from a shower drain, the head, hands and legs finally exposed, imbedded in a concrete-filled stall. A blood-soaked chair had been part of that torture chamber with glow-in-the-dark obscenities painted on the wall. But both Benedict and Coldwater converged at Sunset near the splendor of the mansions which radiated from the Beverly Hills Hotel.

At a point between Canon and the small carp pond at the intersection of Beverly was the house that sickened Lichteiman most on his rare journeys to the office. A small, simple, Spanish home, worth not more than a couple of million. A hedge of oleanders

and a walkway bordered by calla lillies and a basket-
ball hoop above the garage door. Mrs. Janson had
come home after testifying against an Iranian in Los
Angeles Municipal Court, was tied up by a masked
man who made her lie on the floor while he pumped
three bullets into the back of her skull. Her son,
Jamie, handsome and fifteen, returned home to find
his dead mother lying next to a vase of roses and a
burning candle.

Once past the seven hundred block, he was pretty
safe. There weren't many memories of poorer people.
Poor folks committed crimes anyone in the Department could handle: family shoot-outs; holding an
ophthalmologist at bay while drilling a hole in his
wall to get into the Wells Fargo bank; a drug freak
standing nude in front of the Beverly Wilshire Hotel.
These were the usual indiscretions of any small town.

Lichteiman liked to park in the lot next to the
library, just across the street from the Police Department. One section was reserved for Police vehicles,
and, besides, he usually ended up spending more time
in the library than in the offices of the Investigative
Services. Police Headquarters looked more like the
kind of place a Mexican movie star might build. Inside, Lichteiman made his entrance through the Detective Pool, a maze of desks that looked like a
tornado had just ripped through. At this moment he
felt, of all things, a love for his fellow detectives. He
could feel their respect as he waddled his huge body
down the aisle. He'd grunt, smile, listen to a joke from
one of the boys.

But it was Lichteiman's *special* talent that made
them all listen when he spoke, and that "talent" first
became clear in San Francisco many years before.
Lichteiman had been one of eighty detectives added
to the Branchi case when Rose Miller became the sev-

enth victim. Rose had planned on becoming a nun. She was a gentle, caring person who was found one Thanksgiving morning with her throat and breasts slit open. Letters from the killer followed.

"These letters are from some guy who felt he was shit when he was a kid," Lichteiman had said when he'd heard the precinct scuttlebutt. In his San Francisco precinct any unsolicited remark was considered volunteering, and the Lieutenant put him in charge of the paper work, coordinating the lab and shrink reports. "Yeah, maybe his mother did something bad to him . . ."

I HIT A WOMAN ON THE HEAD WITH A HAMMER ONCE, AND I KILLED ANOTHER ONE WITH A WRENCH . . .

"My guess is the old man was never around much, maybe he took off when the kid was born. Then, when his mother hurt him, the kid had nowhere to turn. And he's never forgiven her, the little boy inside him has never forgiven her . . ."

AND GOD'S VOICE TOLD ME TO CUT THEM, TO CUT THEM DEEPLY, DEEPLY.

"Now he's probably married to a loud, bitchy woman . . ."

I FELT AS THOUGH I WAS BEING BATHED IN SEMEN. I WAS LOOKING AT GOD'S SEMEN FROM THE UNIVERSE . . . I HIT THE WOMAN ON THE HEAD SO HARD A PIECE OF HER SKULL FLEW OFF . . .

The Lieutenant and the other detectives were dumbfounded, and so revolted by the content of some of the letters they could barely read them. They were mystified by Lichteiman's immediate understanding of the perverted thoughts and terrifying insanity of the killer. Even the police psychologists bogged down trying to translate the letters into leads and clues.

And when the ripper began to telephone they put Lichteiman on with him because only Lichteiman knew the right things to say, only his voice was soothing to the madman—capable of creating trust. Lichteiman had discussed the most godless details of horror with the ripper as though the subject was irrigation techniques or horticulture. Part of Lichteiman's talent was that he could freely enter the world of a psychopath and live in the world with him. The other part of his talent had to do with a type of "magic" in his mind. Lichteiman could *translate* seemingly mad images into a comprehensible reality.

Lichteiman knew his understanding of a psychopath's mind was based somewhere in his childhood. Always when he worked on such a case the night moves of his own childhood would stir, resonate through time past to the present.

The maniac who had written the letters was in unbearable pain, and that maniac once had been a little boy who had seen things as bad, or even worse, than Lichteiman had. Childhood amnesia had not dulled his own memories: Lichteiman's father beating his mother, threatening to shove a broken bottle into her face; days in family court, his father being subdued by billy clubs as he tried to choke his mother for demanding child support; his mother telling him she wanted to die, that she would take the bus to the Patterson Bridge and . . .

Yes, Lichteiman had understood this ripper in San Francisco. He understood why a boy could hate a mother. He knew the process by which a boy feels inferior, the damage done when a boy can't feel good about himself. Lichteiman had finally taken over the entire San Francisco case, leading the flak-jacketed team in when the ripper had trusted him with one clue too many. He had called Lichteiman, and Lichteiman told him he wanted to meet him. The ripper said he had work to do that night. The ripper had wept, begged to be captured because GOD HAS THE HAMMER IN MY HAND, IT'S IN MY HAND, OH GOD, OH GOD . . .

Lichteiman had heard pounding, a series of metallic thumping noises going on somewhere in the far background at the ripper's end of the line.

"What are those sounds?" Lichteiman had asked.

"They're . . . they're putting up the crucifixes," the killer cried, his voice cracking with terror.

"Crucifixes?"

"Outside my window . . . they're putting up crucifixes. . . . God knows I'm here, and soon it will be my turn . . . first the hammer, then the nails . . ."

The psychologists were confounded, but Lichteiman's mind performed its magic. He *knew* the crucifixes were telephone poles. And within minutes Lichteiman had the telephone company release the three locations in San Francisco where new poles were being pile-driven into place.

Two locations were immediately disqualified as too rural. That night, thanks to Lichteiman, they had their man.

Now, this morning, Lichteiman sat down and began to look through the autopsy reports of what had already been dubbed "the mattress murder." He felt a wave of disgust. By the time he glanced through the photographs, the statements—he felt his disgust turn to apprehension, then a pure chilling fear. There was a madman out there, and as with the many other cases since San Francisco, Lichteiman knew he was destined to play a role. And, if all went well, he and the crazy man would find each other. For a long while he sat in silence, flooded by the horror of what he knew, of what happens in a man's mind when darkness falls.

AUGUST 11

When it grew clearly hopeless, when she knew she was dying, Jack's mother begged to be taken home.

"Jack, let me die in my own house, in my own bed, Jack!"

It was back to Todt Hill Road. She covered her face as the attendants carried her from the ambulance.

"Don't let the neighbors see me!" she sobbed.

Bernice stalked the kitchen. She had never wanted Mom in the hospital, and she hoped Jack was happy now, happy with the biopsy scars, the white rooms, the ghoulish curiosity of the medical students.

"Now she's home," Bernice announced. "And I'm going home too."

Jack's sister roared off toward Ridgefield to make dinner for her husband the engineer, leaving Jack to endure the final hours with the shell of Mrs. Mary Krenner.

"No pills, no more pills," his mother said.

No medicine to keep the heart going, Jack thought. She wants to die.

"I'm frightened, Jack."

He found her crucifix, a huge wooden one, stuck it in her hand, letting her see it. "I hate the church," she had said, year in and year out, for decades. "When I married your father, a priest came to the house and screamed at me that I was not married in the eyes of the Catholic church. People go to church to talk about you. They talk about your clothes. They make fun of you . . ."

Then.

The moment.

Her heart stopped.

"Are you dead, Mother?"

No pulse. No motion. If this were natural death, it would be fine, he thought. Goodbye, Momma. Goodbye. But suddenly his mother's body arched high in the air. It shook, thrashed in seizure, like a *grand mal* fit. Her mouth dropped open. A splash of fluid burst from her mouth. *She's still alive. She's still alive, and now drowning.* Finally, the corpse fell back down on the bed, motionless. *And you brought me here for this. Left me alone for this, my sweet Bernice . . .*

11:15 P.M.

Death. *Death.*

Marjorie had put the children to sleep with a reading of *Bedtime for Francis*, made a cup of tea and resorted to Percodan left over from a root canal episode in February. Now in the darkness of the bedroom she lay waiting for sleep and felt a slight pain in her throat. She couldn't move, and breathing became an effort. At first she thought she was just exhausted from the day, but it was more than likely she was coming down with something. *What have I decided to come down with?* A cough. Courtney had a slight cough before she had gone to sleep. And Danny had complained of a sore throat. Was she really getting sick or was there something especially wrong in her life at the moment?

Oh, this has been some week, I'll tell ya.

Courtney had had another asthma attack. Marjorie vividly remembered the first attack, the hospital, her little girl's chest, pushing up and down, the oxygen tent. Poor Courtney in that bed at Cedars Sinai, puffing, *poor Courtney and there's nothing I can do.* The all night vigil. The recovery. The joyous flowers from the gift shop with the big balloons. *Keep her home whenever she looks run down. I'll stop it. It'll never happen to her again. Never.*

But it did.

And the second attack came when Jack had been out to a playwrights meeting in the San Fernando Valley. Before it got too late she called the doctor. Don't get nervous, he had said. He'll call back in an hour and check. If she wakes up gasping, she'll need the Theodur. If only Jack had been home to calm her. Then the unthinkable. She had picked up the phone and it was dead. She had seen Jack hooking up some of his electronic equipment to the phone during the day and she just knew he had screwed up the wiring. Now she was cut off from the world and had to run across the street to Mercer's house and call the doctor. He said to bring Courtney into the office. There he gave her a shot of adrenalin—then another. Back home again she started to breathe easier, but after that came Marjorie's own exhaustion, the same exhaustion she felt now. The exhaustion on behalf of her family.

An hour later, still awake, she decided to go down to the kitchen and make herself a cup of Brim. While waiting for the water to boil she decided to put a load of wash in, and finally got a handle on what was really bothering her. Jack's coldness and distance on their anniversary *had* disappointed her. In a way it was a reminder of the Jack she knew before they had married—the one Marjorie Hilden, approaching thirty, her ovaries aging, had fallen in love with. Oh, she had been going out with a few men, but there was nobody special. She had kept waiting for the feeling. She had kept thinking her life was going to begin soon. That's how her twenties had disappeared. This waiting to share. That was the first loneliness. The second loneliness came when she met Jack and began to date him; soon they lived together on Eighth Street, in the Georgetown Plaza. When they broke up three months later she was alone again, and it was even more painful because she still loved him. She'd walk along Eighth Street and look up at his window in the southeast corner of the twenty-third floor. She prayed that he would appear magically and look down and see her walking along. She had dreams in which he would rush down in the elevator to catch her and beg her forgiveness. Jack Krenner. He had a play running at the time, and had started writing his first screenplay. Of course she had jobs of her own. At the Chicago Summer Theatre where they had met. At a PR firm in Newark. Other jobs. But then, after breaking up with Jack, she was without a career, and between worlds. She wanted out of business and into the arts. She had tried writing a screenplay, several pages every day, while holding down a job at the fundraising department of the Bowery Street Settlement. It was a dangerous subway ride back to her small one-room apartment on Sixteenth Street. There was a period of sorting through her own neurotic history: her mother's expectations of her, and then her mother's death when she was only fifteen. Looking back, she realized she had had no concept of the real world. She didn't know how to do simple things. Her mother had done everything for her, had never taught her how to act. She didn't know how to make decisions. She'd never had to make one. This was the time Marjorie had to learn what she wanted. Who was Marjorie Hilden?

She had been engaged twice before. Once in 1973 and again in '74, all part of the saga which had brought her to Chicago. But then she believed destiny had brought Jack Krenner to her. Her publicity job for the Summer Theatre was to book him on the radio shows, television, drive him around. Being with him sparked something in her. She liked him, responded to him. It was a time for her to be born again. Jack Krenner, free spirit, impulsive, lonely.

The fight when she had told him off: "The only time you touch me is when we're in bed, Jack. Any other time you don't reach out to me. And if I reach out to you, you turn to stone. I find that very frustrating, Jack. I'm very warm and affectionate. I want to kiss and hold onto you. I don't quite know what to do."

"Then get out!" he had screamed at her.

And out she had gone, back to another loneliness. And this loneliness, the second one, hurt terribly. She began to pray that he would take her back. She would find a way with him. She would be satisfied with their skin fusing hot and complete only in the bed. She would bear the coolness of the days knowing she would be in his warmth for the nights.

AUGUST 13

After the funeral he drove to Manhattan and checked into a cheap midtown hotel, planning to fly home the next morning. As he lay on the ugly bed in the ugly room, he could feel a wire inside him snapping, a final wire which had been holding him. Within one moment Time became unbearable, dreadful. For hours he fell, lower, deeper until his mind heard a *voice*. It was the same voice he had first heard in a cab several years before—a night when one of his plays had opened and there had been some very bad feelings inside him. At this moment it didn't matter to him if the voice was coming from a dream or a conscious drifting. He had sensed the voice had been a part of him since a child. He and the voice had been children together and became one during The Trauma, as his mother dragged his manhood to the glowing flame.

CHAPTER FOUR

It was almost midnight in L.A. when Marjorie got his call. Yes, she and the kids would pick him up the next evening, American Airlines. "I'm sorry, my darling, about your mother. I *am* sorry." She felt like calling him back the moment she hung up. She wanted to be with him and hold him. It would be 3:00 A.M. his time. Where had he been until 3:00 in the morning? Perhaps he was depressed, a few drinks, Joe Allen's Bar with a friend. She should have gone with him.

She watched the ocean mist roll into the neighborhood. From the front window of her work room, she could see a light in the doctor's massive, dark brick house across the street. It was a soft moving light. The doctor was watching television, she decided. He had servants, an operating room, anesthesia, perhaps drugs. Some night there would be a crash, glass breaking, she imagined. A car load of young drug addicts breaking in before he finished the wall. The finished wall would be electrified. Would the lights automatically go on at dusk? How many exterior television cameras?

She turned back to the typewriter, pushing her novel further. Her young heroine was at dinner with her imaginary father. He would give her advice, hope. "Don't be so impatient," her father said in a gentle voice. "You relax with me because you know I love you. But one of these days a boy will come along and see all the beautiful things I see. He'll be a prince, and he's going to love you the rest of your life . . ."

Click!

Clunk!

Sounds again. It had to be a raccoon on the roof, she decided. Or perhaps they were even noises from her writer's mind.

Damn!

Out of paper.

Crunch! Click!

O.K., O.K., she thought, a raccoon or a possum. Something moving from the roof gutters to the trees. She got up and went out into the hall, half expecting to see rats running along the rug border.

Nothing.

She checked on the kids sleeping. They were safe. On the wall in Courtney's room was the plaster hand impression she had made when she and Danny were in Miss Mandrell's group at the Coldwater Canyon nursery school. Marjorie could never pass it without feeling angry about Miss Mandrell's unprofessional behavior that spring. Miss Mandrell was the head teacher at the nursery school and had called her and Jack down to tell them she thought Danny had dyslexia.

He was being put in the lowest pre-reading group. He was being stigmatized. Miss Mandrell had not warned them that most of the parents of the kids in nursery school had already bought phonics books, had hired tutors for their children. Already most of the native parents had totally planned out the lives of their children, that they would go from Beverly Hills Canyon Nursery School to Buckley, or to Harvard Boys School in the Valley, and then on to the real Harvard or Yale. And Miss Mandrell told them she was very, very frightened for Danny, that he seemed so slow. "Oh very sweet and cute and nice," she said, "nice boy, but off in a dream world just like his sister Courtney. And if there's some family history of dyslexia, you had better begin the testing now." Marjorie and Jack had gone through the roof after spending eight hundred dollars to find out that Danny was absolutely normal, and actually superior, *considerably* superior in intelligence. They could hardly wait until that June, when little Danny put on his cap and gown and graduated.

From the kids' rooms, Marjorie went to check the far hallway. Then down the main staircase through the living room. She'd left the floodlights on in the rose garden. Whenever Jack went away, she lit up the house like a Christmas tree. She would have to parade in front of the four huge sliding glass doors of the living room and then into the massive fishbowl of the library. Sam roused himself from the kitchen. She heard his reluctant trot as he came out to escort her. If anyone were hiding out behind the eucalyptus trees or in the jungle of ivy near the tennis court, they'd see her with the Great Dane, and they'd move on to plunder some other house.

She knew Jack kept his typing paper in the top left hand drawer of his immense brown desk. She flipped on a gooseneck lamp, and took out several sheets. She'd buy more tomorrow. She was amused at how guilty she felt, like an intruder. She looked around his place of work: the IBM typewriter, the massive walls of books stretching from the white marble fireplace to the collection of scripts. For a moment she sat in one of the old but expensive Italian leather chairs gathered around a huge, stainless-steel coffee table. She looked across to the awards and the army of framed photos. His mother in a raccoon coat on some football field, a picture of him with Danny in

Australia, another of her with Courtney in Connecticut. A publicity photo of the four of them surrounded by toys. She caught herself deliberately lingering at his bulletin board, the collage of pinioned names, phone numbers, magic marker messages: *Go beyond yourself. Shakespeare clicked into evil beyond himself. Villains think they are right.* Small paintings of surrealistic landscapes, ornate balloons, old fighter planes. The books on the desk: psychiatry tomes, books on quotations, literary construction. And his journals, years of recorded dreams, ideas, hopes. He had been on his way to becoming a dramatic and literary force years before she'd even dreamed of being anybody—years before she had been *allowed* to dream of being anybody. She stood and went to a large new journal and found herself peering into it: *Caffeine problem. My sister is four years ahead of me. What happens to her, happens to me. A cauldron in my stomach. I put a cap on it. Believed there would be no consequences. Last night I lost sight. Lost speech. My legs went out from under me. Mount Sinai Emergency Room. I thought I had a tumor on my brain, a purple line coming from my hairline to the top of my right eye. I wish I was never born. . . .* As she read on she wished he was in her arms so she could rock him and touch him and tell him everything was going to be so fine.

AUGUST 14
2:00 P.M.

Marjorie herded the kids into the Seville and hurried to meet Jack's plane. At the airport, she had time to dash with them to a bathroom for a glance in a mirror. Noticing a few gray hairs invading her bangs, she decided to have them dyed; but she was thankful the rest of her hair was black and glossy. She caught herself protruding her chin slightly, trying to make it look stronger; and she held in her belly, always worrying people could tell there were stretch marks on her abdomen.

Jack looked haggard when he came off the plane. She kissed him, tried to buoy his spirits while keeping the kids from grabbing his legs or yanking at his luggage. Danny ripped open his present, a Frogger video game, which caused him to literally jump up and down. Courtney found her unwrapped doll in a shopping bag Jack had carried on the plane, and began hugging its blood-velvet gown. Marjorie held Jack's hand proudly as they all boarded the motorized walkway. Strangers smiled at them. She knew what the folks were seeing: wife, arm-in-arm with husband, children with gorgeous hair and perfect toys. A happy family.

Jack made love to her that night. He entered her slowly, deeply, his organ enlarging to dimensions she thought impossible. He pinioned her, penetrating so completely she was certain she would be damaged, but her body only urged him on into her narrow tunnel, undisturbed by two childbirths, her body clamping and releasing in a way she hadn't known in the seven years of their marriage.

Marjorie fell asleep in his arms.

She woke up just before three in the morning, and reached out for him. He wasn't there. She was only half awake when she heard the horrible footsteps. The night lights from the garden reflected off the eucalyptus and grandiflora trees, creating menacing forms on the walls. The footsteps were coming faster now, heavier. Some monstrous emissary of Satan was about to burst in upon her. She wouldn't be able to dial for help. There wouldn't be time to scream. Why wasn't Sam barking?

A racing shadow appeared at the threshold, darted across the room, and leaped into her mother's arms. It was only Courtney. Her movements had all been magnified into thunder by the intercom above the headboard. Marjorie always had the volume turned up high enough to hear even Courtney's sleeping breath.

"I had a bad dream," Courtney gasped.

"What was it about?"

"I don't know," she said, snuggling into the warmth of her mother's body. "A man was after me. I was running in the backyard and a blue man was after me and I tried to get up the jungle gym but he got my legs and he was hurting me and I fell on the cement and he was hurting my dollies . . ."

"Nobody's after you."

"Yes, he was. And he had my hair, he was pulling my hair . . ."

In a few minutes Courtney was sound asleep again, but Marjorie stayed awake listening to her daughter's breathing. It was regular. Fine. Just fine. She had bad dreams once a week or so, but never cried. Courtney, the brave. Marjorie enjoyed teaching her children that the night was good. That wonderful things happened when you sleep. We need to dream. We need it. The good dreams and the bad. *Our dreams prepare us . . .*

Marjorie decided to get out of bed and go down for something to drink. She went to the center hall stairs, and down to the lower foyer. The living room was empty. A crack of light at the foot of the library door told her Jack was at work.

She didn't want to disturb him, and continued on to the kitchen. She opened the refrigerator and decided to dilute half a glass of grapefruit juice with soda water. Something made her check the milk.

Again, *the foul odor.* This time stronger. As the carton gurgled its contents into the Disposall, Marjorie vowed to change supermarkets. Some lazy, unconscionable truck driver or packer was letting the milk sit in the sun on some loading platform. It hadn't been left out at home, unless Jack had taken it out *hours* before and it went bad very quickly, and then he had put the container back . . .

She took her drink, and decided to step out onto the cement patio. She began to stroll around the pool. She found herself moving through the far shadows of the yard, checking on the rabbits in their cage by the back fence. Good, they had food pellets and water. At least Maria was remembering to feed the things. She moved on to the low stone wall to find the rose garden.

Marjorie had slowly begun to learn the flora of Beverly Hills. Most of it was so beautiful and exotic that she was motivated for the first time in her life to tell the difference between magnolia blossoms and margaritas, the sweet scent of a lemon tree and the gorgeous perfume of a lime. She had begun to distinguish between a Eureka rose and a Chrysler. To differentiate between the various shades of bougainvillea.

A faint wind stirred, some small animals scurried in the ivy at a distance. Marjorie wondered why she suddenly felt guilty. She was only taking some air. She had every right to be in her own backyard at this hour. Then she realized why she had drifted to the far corner of the property, near the tennis court. From here she could look across the full length of the yard and see the entire house. The kitchen windows, the glass of the sunroom addition, the night-lights along the main upper and lower hallway. She could also see Jack at his desk in the library, and knew he couldn't see her outside in the darkness. She watched him for several minutes as though viewing a mime show. He was speaking into a tape recorder. It all made for a handsome diorama, the walls of books, the hanging plants. She knew he appreciated the extra effort she'd made in decorating *his* room. And he was wearing the Superdad nightshirt, which was what he had to be to pay their awesome mortgage. She was about to slide back toward the house unseen when she noticed him moving to a shelf. Perhaps he was reaching for another cassette, scotch tape, a pen. He took something from behind a shelf of oversized books. A plastic bag. Then, for the first time, Marjorie saw Jack using cocaine.

AUGUST 15
7:30 A.M.

Marjorie woke up, washed her face, went to the kitchen and made a pot of fresh-ground coffee in the Melitta. She heard the maid stirring in her room, then stepped out to get the *Times* which had been tossed under an azalea bush. When the coffee had brewed she poured herself a cup and automatically added some milk. It had that sickening, unhealthy odor again—like something dead. Another container of milk, spoiled.

When the maid came out, Marjorie asked her about it. "Maria, the milk is sour again."

"Sour?" she inquired in her heavy Mexican accent. Maria was barely thirty, but already looked like an old woman. She was short, dark, her long black hair pulled back into a ponytail.

"That's right."

"It can't be. Got it yesterday."

"Well, it *is*!"

Maria shrugged.

"Maybe you buy old milk."

"I checked the date, Maria. But I was thinking perhaps you don't baggie your garlic and herbs as well as you could. Perhaps that's the problem."

"Maybe Danny and Court . . ."

"They can't *reach* the milk, Maria."

"No es cosa mia."

Marjorie had to smile as she watched Maria open another gallon of milk and lean over to sniff it. The bulk of her ponytail fell down the back of her white uniform.

"This one good."

"Yes, Maria," Marjorie agreed. "It's only the opened ones that seem to go sour . . ."

9:00 A.M.

When he first woke up, he reached across the bed to let Marjorie know that he needed her contact. That this time he was really going to try. His fingertips touched crumpled sheets, and he realized she must be already down in the kitchen giving orders for the day, making coffee, getting the kids organized. He lay his head back on the pillow, and the swelling of his penis reminded him of the sex the evening before.

He was cheered when he arrived in the kitchen. Kisses from Marjorie and hugs from Court and Danny, who both held on to him for dear life.

"Don't go away again, Daddy, don't go away."

"I won't, Court."

"I got some white splotches on my hand from touching a lobster on Saturday," Danny bragged.

"Marjorie," Jack said, "I need some clothes. Socks."

"You should get some new slacks, too. Bullocks'

and Robinsons' are having sales. If you go could you take Court—I mean, when you've finished your writing. She'd love being with her Daddy, wouldn't you Court?"

"Can I go can I go can I can I?"

"Yes, darling."

"Oh, and Jack, you got a call from Niko Aris' office. They want you to take a meeting on Wednesday."

By ten he was driving their white Volvo station wagon west along Santa Monica Boulevard. Court was singing. *Now I know my alphabet, tell me what a good girl I am.* At every stop light he gave her a hug and she flirted with him. She rattled on, nonstop. *Let's go to the park. Push on the swings, Daddy. Danny punched me, I went over to Nora's house. Buy me a toy. Can I have some bubble gum? Take a little girl through your window. Tell me what a good girl I am.* Singing, clapping, stamping.

He finally had to tune her out. He began to realize that he should have taken some cocaine with him. His plan had been to cut his doses to six times a day, but obviously the morning wasn't a good time to do it. He could take two lines in the morning, and then another after lunch, and then only three after dinner. Then if things got too rough, if he had to crash into bed and the nightmares came, well—he'd see.

The subtext of the morning began to play back to him, but he tried to tell himself everything was fine. *What's going on between Marjorie and me*, he told himself, *is healthy conflict. Good old healthy conflict. So what if sometimes I feel something's wrong? It's only a salubrious insecurity.* At least that was the cocaine line, the cocaine full-dosage catechism. But now, in this instant in the car, something else was happening.

Cracks in his consciousness revealed patterns he thought he had left behind years before.

"The ticket, the ticket," Court shouted.

Jack slowed the car. He held Court's little body out of the window so she could reach the dispensing machine at the parking garage below the Century City Mall. Ticket in hand, she squealed with joy as a bell rang and a gate lifted to allow entry. He didn't want to disturb her, he didn't want her to know what was going on inside him. He would try very, very hard to fight it. He would struggle and win. He would talk aloud now so she wouldn't know anything was wrong. *We're going to shop and Daddy's going to buy pants because Daddy has some important meetings and Daddy's going to write a movie and we're going to have a good time and get very rich.* He knew if his tone remained normal, she wouldn't suspect, wouldn't be afraid. He would pretend he was reading the comics or waiting for Mommie to come out of McDonald's with shakes and quarter-pounders, or counting the minutes until Disneyland opened. *I'm going to buy Court chocolate chips and candy ladies and blue carnations, and . . .*

He would have to go out soon. He would take his gym bag, and he'd even remember a towel and a change of shirt—and he'd smile and just tell Marjorie he was going to work out . . .

Suddenly he noticed Court smiling at him.

"What are you thinking about, honey?"

"I was just wondering, Daddy—did Grandma look very pretty in her coffin?"

11:15 A.M.

After her work for the morning, Marjorie decided to drive down to do a little shopping. Sliding into the Seville, she found the button she wanted among the profusion of gadgets under the dashboard. The garage door opened. She backed the Seville out, pulling it parallel with the house. She knew Jack loved gadgets, but she had been somewhat surprised when he went and had a telephone and other electronic equipment installed in the Cadillac. She didn't know what half of it was, but she did know they really couldn't afford it all. There were more tape decks and CB-looking gizmos than the back of a Mercedes limo she had seen once. The chauffeur had chatted with her, telling her it belonged to Sammy Davis Jr., and that only two people in the world had the same model. The other was the Pope.

Maybe they were security devices, Marjorie thought. She wondered if they would ever build a wall around their property, as all their neighbors had.

Yes. If we had more money, Jack would want a wall.

Lights to run the full length of the property. Two TV cameras to spy, warn.

A Lincoln was coming toward her down Lost Orchard. This would be Miss Maggie, the aging blond star whose mansion squatted to the right of the property. Miss Maggie waved, but Marjorie remembered the star's words to her the first week they'd moved in: *"Hello, I thought you'd better know that in this neighborhood we do not visit to call each other. We respect privacy."*

Marjorie pulled around the cement triangle where Los Orchard merged with Valley Road. The whole canyon had once been a silent movie star's estate. Across the street was the plastic surgeon's brick monster of a home. Large sweaty workmen held tightly to a large, pounding machine which looked like an outsized pogo stick. Above its thumping soared high-pitched sounds like bats squeaking. Tarpaulins snapped. Mexicans scurried near the doctor's tennis court as though excavating some antiquity. The next house up on Valley Road was that of Mercer, the producer—and next to him was a stucco home owned by the Hutchinses, a strange old couple with an authentic English garden and carp pond. Several swimming-pool service trucks were lined up along the street, tree workers snipping, axes cutting. Lilies of the Nile moved their delicate necks in a swift morning breeze. Someone was jogging, running swiftly with a sense of urgency. After months of living there Marjorie was getting the homes clear in her mind. On the left, Iranians lived in a pink home with an obelisk, and on the right lived G. Frankel, a sitcom actor whose shows were in reruns. His pack of Dobermans was always pacing, snarling behind his towering electric gates. Down on the right was the leading man from the spy thrillers, a cottage bought for 1.6 million, and on the left now was a loud, desperate actress who loved to appear on talk shows and pretend she was sleeping with the entire Israeli army. A Chicano with one arm rode in a truck filled with desperate faces, the servant horde of illegal aliens hired to feed the powerful and wealthy of upper Coldwater Canyon. But Marjorie reminded herself that she was only passing through. She would never become part of this, she would fight it, and her soul would always be with Central Park and Rumpelmayers and Serendipity.

She reached the crest, where Valley Road hit Coldwater. A black Ferrari screeched and swerved toward her, almost sideswiping her Seville. She'd seen the face: some stoned kid from the other end of Lost Orchard. His license plate: SEX 4U.

Starting down Coldwater on the left side were two homes which had been for sale for over three years. Both were made of white stucco with no windows facing onto the heavy traffic. They looked like German bunkers, even after the architect had added several matching terraces in an attempt to soften their monumental starkness.

Marjorie smiled. The homes on the downside of the hill featured odd mailboxes that always delighted Danny and Courtney. Some of the mailboxes were shaped like animals. A swan. A dove. One was a large donkey. Another was an exact duplicate of the home itself. Still another was modeled after the House of the Seven Gables.

Marjorie drove past Sassoon's home which was just across the street from Coldwater Nursery School and the jogging field. Once, not long after the Sassoon marriage had exploded, Marjorie swore she had seen Beverly and Eric Estrada jogging together at sunset. The last she had heard the Sassoon home was on the market for over six million.

From Shadow Hill Way on, the opulence of Beverly Hills could not be denied. From the very first turn at Lexington, each home had a legend as large as its structure. A massive two-story brick home behind a brick wall on the left had been built for the Shah of Iran's sister. Here the gates and walls made those of Lost Orchard Road look rather frail. Several of the estates were the length of an entire block. The biggest had once belonged to the head of a movie studio before he had gone broke.

There were so many bars on the windows of Beverly Hills homes that they began to look rather ornamental. The poor in the surrounding towns of Los Angeles grew more desperate with every year. Robberies in Beverly Hills had skyrocketed. It didn't help that each mansion had a back yard that faced a service road designed to keep garbage out of sight and allow access for groundskeepers. Those same back alleyways also provided ideal access for burglars. As a result, security precautions had become a neighborhood obsession, and Marjorie had begun to accept the bars and the walls as part of the landscape.

Their next door neighbor Mercer had had her and Jack over for a barbeque when they first moved into Lost Orchard Road. "I have hand grenades," Mr. Mercer had told them, quite seriously. "If anyone comes near my house, and I feel he is in any way a threat to my being or my property, he's going to get blasted with a grenade. Frankel up the street has five killer Dobermans, but I've got shotguns, handguns, a semi-automatic weapon, an electric bullhorn, an automatic rifle, and I take lessons twice a month on weapons use. We have an arsenal. Of course my wife only knows how to use mace. Also after ten at night, anything you touch in the yard is liable to give you an electric shock that could fry you. After midnight you could get ripped to pieces on my grounds. And the reason I've guarded my house so well is that I don't want anyone hurt. That's what we all do here. We take precautions to guard our homes. To let the bad guys know that this is not going to be a profitable venture. Those of us who are really defending ourselves never get attacked. They know we'll blow their heads off."

OCTOBER 1
10:45 a.m.

Jack heard tapping on one of the glass windows of the library. He looked up to see Danny, smiling, bright-eyed, beckoning him like a pint-sized devil to come outside. Jack loved this little prince of a boy, his boy, his *son*, and he was aware this child was more handsome than either he or Marjorie had ever been. Actually both Danny and Courtney were so startlingly beautiful, Jack often joked that a martian must have landed and fertilized Marjorie while she slept.

"Can I show you my mud hut?" Danny wanted to know, miming behind the glass.

"You bet," Jack said, sliding back the door and stepping out onto the cement ribbon which bordered the back lawn. Beyond the grass was a short rise of ivy that blended into eucalyptus trees and a thicket of bougainvillea and wisteria. Far to the right, the cement walk led to the tennis court.

"This is a *secret*," Danny whispered, leading the way across the grass.

"Of course."

Jack was really pleased Danny was willing to share whatever it was with him. Most of Danny's activities he kept to himself. He would only give hints about what had gone on at camp or school. In fact, Jack knew it was only Danny's sense of privacy which had led to that rather unfortunate diagnosis by the nursery school their first year in California.

Danny had never minded talking about any of his small failures, but his successes were usually top secret. If he had gotten all his spelling words right on a test, if he had been picked to star in the Ugly Duckling play or had advanced from a slower reading group to a faster—these matters he would hide. He also hid any tooth that fell out, but this, Jack had decided, was simply a test to see if the tooth fairy would still leave silver dollars. Marjorie had always insisted on *three* silver dollars, assorted change, and a package of Trident gum—which Jack thought terribly extravagant.

Jack lifted his gaze from the thicket. He could barely make out the form of his son sitting on top of the rust-wood fence which prevented passage into Miss Maggie's yard. He seemed to be suspended, floating behind a waterfall of ivy and great blue flower trumpets.

"Wow! That's terrific!" Jack puffed, his voice full of loving praise.

"Come around the side," Danny ordered.

"Okay."

The igloo of leaves gave way on the left and Jack could see his son in the shadows of the hut. By now Samson and Sandy had lifted themselves from sunning near the pool and crashed upon the site, flanking Danny as though they were hired henchmen. Samson stood as tall as Danny—with his great drooling black head and white-crested chest. Sandy was only half as big.

"Why do you want a mud hut?" Jack wanted to know. "I never saw a kid with a mud hut!"

"Protection."

"*Protection?*"

"Yes."

"What kind of protection?"

"From people."

Jack noticed a small piece of wood missing from the fence in back of the hut. "You've got to keep that fixed," he started to point, when Samson moved, growled.

"Okay, Daddy."

Jack looked at the dogs still flanking his son. For a moment he felt as though they were actually *guarding* Danny in his little mud house. They seemed to be playing the game, too.

"It's your job to make sure there's no holes in the fence," Jack stressed.

"Yes, Daddy. Do you like all my mud balls?"

Danny pointed to a line up of about thirty dirt-mud balls about the size of oranges.

"I can throw them, Daddy," Danny bragged. He picked one up, stepped out of the hut and hurled it at the broad bark of a eucalyptus trunk. The ball fell apart in air, but a sizable chunk hit the tree and stuck firm.

"Great."

"One of my mud balls has a rock and a worm in it."

"Terrific."

OCTOBER 3
MORNING

Jack had a harder day than usual. He had to finish preparing to pitch a story to ABC about the healing of a woman alcoholic, and find a way of lifting the material above the threadbare. By eleven that morning he had to Xerox three copies of a thriller proposal and deliver them to Warner Brothers in Burbank. His agent, Gilda Heyler, expected him at eleven-thirty. At two-thirty he was due at Niko Aris' house for a poolside meeting to discuss the second draft of Jack's only paying project, *Hold Me, Touch Me.* Again he felt dangerously close to overload.

When Jack Krenner had moved to Beverly Hills with his wife and kids the year before, he thought he had left Manhattan and all its problems behind. An incident in a Central Park playground had been the last straw. A drunk had wandered into the children's playground at 67th Street (he happened to be black, and really quite frightening) and he had decided to urinate near a sandbox where Courtney and Danny were playing along with several other kids. Some of the children had been brought to the park by Spanish or Jamaican nannies, but there were enough other fathers so that when Jack yelled at the drunk who had drifted from urinating to flashing at the kids—and finally to actual masturbation—Jack was shocked to find he had no support.

"I've got a gun and I'm going to shoot your head off," the drunk had threatened him.

"I'm getting the cops," Jack had told him, and started off toward Fifth Avenue.

"I *am* a cop," the guy kept yelling. "I'm a cop and I'll shoot your head off, you lousy cocksucker. You *cocksuckerrr*!"

When he had finally gotten the cops to come, Jack found none of the other parents would press charges. It was Jack alone who had to get into a patrol car, the drunk in another, and go downtown to start the process of pressing charges. The "process" consisted of the drunk being released in less than three hours, while Jack had to stay *five* hours before being able to give his deposition in the witness holding room. Part of the delay was the arrival of Mayor Koch who came down with complete TV coverage because the mayor himself had been assaulted with eggs while giving a speech near the Plaza.

It had taken a while longer for Jack Krenner to arrange the move to L.A. There was the matter of finding the right kind of assignment and of shaking himself loose from a three-year lease at 25 Central

Park West. And even after a year of living in Beverly Hills, he knew Marjorie hadn't wanted to leave New York. He knew she had done it only because she loved him so totally, and even that nagged at him. She was at his side, helping him make the decisions that would be best for him—not for her. There were moments when they would eat in one of L.A.'s terrible delicatessens and he could tell she was secretly sighing for a real roast beef sandwich from Wolf's, or they'd be out strolling after a salad bar meal at R.J.'s and he'd know she yearned to be walking along 57th Street. He had seen other transplanted wives so disgruntled and selfish they made their marriages shake as though they were on the San Andreas fault. At parties, other wives would lead long arguments about how much more alive they had felt in New York. They'd always say how much better New York culture, people, theater was. The store windows, they said, had ideas, and spirit, and the shock of the new. But Marjorie, his wife, filtered her longing. Her needs were secondary to his. She had allowed that, encouraged that out of her love for him. She lived for him, to help him be the man, the father—to step in and fight alongside him with a sense of all his fears and hopes and dreams.

Rain and darkness too, she'll not complain . . .

"Where's the rape?" turned out to be the only question Niko Aris seemed to know. Jack would tell him a plot, and it wasn't long into the first draft that he realized the producer didn't know how to handle dramatic materials. Whenever he'd catch Niko in a flagrant perversion of plotting, Jack would try to teach him the ins and outs of drama. "Our heroine needs *heart*," Jack tried to explain. "We've got to understand *why* she drinks. We need to know who the people are, what the relationships are; their conflict; there has to be a major character decision."

"Bullshit," Aris had said after the first few weeks of dramatic pretension faded. "Look, I know ass, tits and sand. We start with the mother getting raped in a flashback, end with the daughter getting raped. It makes a nice sandwich. And I want a freeze on boobs during the end credits. Remember Bo Derek in *Tarzan*. The film was a piece of shit but the audience stayed in their seats until the last credit rolled over her tits."

In the East Jack had felt more like a husband. In California he found it a harder battle to take his kids to the zoo or down to a movie. He'd finish his morning work, but then the phone would ring and he'd have to take a meeting with a new producer or pitch a story idea to Fox or ABC. Often the story he pitched would be one variation on his life with Marjorie and the kids. "You see, folks," he'd perform for a room full of blank, unbelievably young studio executives. "This is a story about a family we all know. They're great people with great kids. There's Richard, a Dick Benjamin type, serious, intense—who's a CPA for a business management firm that handles a group like Kiss. And he's married to Susan, who's like Paula Prentiss, and she's attractive, nice dark hair and a smile—she's down to earth, endearingly disjointed, absentminded and vulnerable—but in a crisis she can be a lion. See, that's the whole series. The husband is usually the lion, but in a crisis he disintegrates. This is a series about survival in the eighties! This is filled with all the identifiable problems even a family in Topeka will recognize. Every week we'll handle a problem like interest rates, the Moral Majority, the price of food, singles, teenage sex—all of it! And the opening credits will be in sepia, like in *Murder on the Orient Express* . . ."

Like, like, like . . .

But nobody was buying.

Gilda—a darling-looking yenta of a woman, not quite five feet tall—had become his main confidante in California. Of course, he couldn't tell her everything—certainly nothing which might portray him as disabled or mentally unfit to fulfill any assignment which might come along. But he'd discuss things with her like the myth of the perfect family. After one of his more potent arguments with Marjorie, he'd usually call Gilda and take her to lunch. She had been a great help guiding him past some of the new obstacles in the fast lane of the town. She had always encouraged him to tell Marjorie how he felt about things, not to hide his feelings so much from his family.

"If you're scared about death or bills or a heart attack, tell her," she said. "And don't lay any trips on your kids. Let your kids spin their own dreams and stop insisting they behave like adult midgets."

There were moments of great paranoia for him in the marriage, Gilda knew, but she still felt they were mostly normal fantasies which floated through every husband's night and were not part of madness. Once, in his lowest depths, he had complained to her about the marriage, it was so predictable that he and Marjorie were getting up every morning at the same time, doing the very same things, his wife was even writing like he did. Even the breakfast foods were too predictable. Gilda knew that once a month he'd just get drunk and wonder what the hell was he still married for? What were they all still *living* for? But then she'd remind him that most of his misery was the mounting pain that he was nearly broke—but a new assignment would be along soon, she'd keep telling him.

Gilda Heyler came to the office every day wearing huge custom-tinted glasses, her hair piled high on her head in such an extreme tightness she looked like she was constantly forced to smile. She wore blouses which were too transparent and delicate for a woman of fifty years of age, and she would openly brag about having the legs of a twenty-year-old starlet. She delighted in keeping exact records of clients: where she sent them, where they had victories, and where they were shot down. Clients who didn't carry their weight for six months were automatically dropped, unless they were good-looking actors or writers. Jack had known her earlier in New York. She was younger, very wild and drawing attention to herself at Village parties by doing things like greeting a friend with rather startling embraces. She would leap at a guy, grab onto his neck and wrap her legs around his waist. She was also known to jump into Jacuzzis with seven guys, and it was only her big-boned and owlish face which prevented her from being raped. Her behavior was considered hilarious, not sexy. She was more "one of the boys" than anything, and more than once the rumor ran about that she was a lesbian. By the time Jack found her again in California she had toned completely down, and they rarely alluded to her early shenanigans. Gilda had learned how to play the game, and she played it with the best.

Jack felt comfortable in Gilda's office. He admired the brown weave wallpaper, the earth tones of the carpet and ceiling, and the polished wood desk and shelving. It had taken him longer than expected to Xerox that morning, and his delivery to Warner Brothers had turned out to be a problem when the front guard wouldn't let him park in the oval front of the Administration Building. That had meant a long walk from Pass Avenue, and then there had been traffic on Highland Avenue as he tried to get back to Beverly Hills. Now with Gilda, for some strange reason, he had let his conversation drift toward the very personal instead of staying on the track, the plan to get a star into at least a summer run of his play. If she could stay sober and sane she would take it around the New England straw hat circuit. Jack knew it would mean up to five thousand dollars a week for him, enough to pay bills until he could land a second movie. But he had strayed from the deadlines of booking Westport, and Cape Cod, and Algonquin, Maine, and he found himself talking about male menopause. He was talking about feeling very depressed and very old, and about his last birthday when someone had given him a walking stick. His fortieth birthday, and he had gotten a cane! And Marjorie had given him a gift certificate for an aerobics class—it was supposed to be better than Jane Fonda's place and the Anatomy Asylum—but he had come home depressed when he had seen most of the class consisted of chorus boys and the exercises were like rehearsals for a Broadway musical. A typist he had been using gave him a copy of an LP of the Sex Knights, a punk-rock group he had never heard of, and the typist had asked Jack where had he been! This was a hot group; should she have gotten him the Ink Spots or the Mills Brothers?

Gilda had laughed. That was her wonderful talent; she could completely sympathize with a client and still have a good howl about it. And it wasn't cruelty. Her laughter was infectious and delicious. It provided a release which always seemed to put the world back into perspective.

"It's rough turning forty in this town," she told him. "I'm the only woman or man I know who's middle-aged in this business and hasn't had a first face lift."

She had made him a mug of herbal tea, and swiveled in the chair behind her desk. She went into detail about a dozen guys in the agency who had gone off the deep end because they had found themselves middle-aged and realized they weren't going to be moving up in the company.

"Their kids didn't need them anymore," Gilda said. "Their liberated wives no longer focussed their lives exclusively around them. They run around the agency here with this *who am I? What's going to happen to me?* look on their faces. It happens to all of them."

CHAPTER FIVE

OCTOBER 17
2:00 A.M.

The alley was blocked off with wood barricades, and a dozen vehicles blasted their headlights from their position on Camden Drive. Squad cars, two ambulances, two unmarked sedans—and Lichteiman's old Cadillac—illuminated the scene within.

Lichteiman moved slowly past the barricades, accepted the salute of a patrolman. He could tell from the way the other detectives had removed themselves from the body that something very unpleasant was waiting. The first report on his car radio had mentioned only that it was a young woman. On the body were marks suggestive of a recent mastectomy, leading to preliminary thoughts that the death was a suicide. Camden wasn't that far from Cedars of Sinai Hospital. And there were other cases of patients who had undergone surgery and come out of anesthesia wanting to kill themselves. In Beverly Hills, the sudden loss of physical beauty was considered motive for self-destruction.

"Her breasts are cut off. I don't know what the hell it is," Straub said, watching the coroner's crew go over the body. He took out a cigarette from his inside pocket and lit it. Lichteiman went closer, knelt down.

"Excuse me," Lichteiman wheezed, and even the head examiner made way.

"What? She have an operation?" Straub wanted to know.

"Give me your flashlight."

"No marks on the skull," Detective Tolman offered. "Just her chest. . . ."

Lichteiman moved his light slowly down the naked form, checking for depressions, bruises.

"Maybe Sinai. Maybe she was at Sinai and flipped out when she saw what she looked like after the mastectomy . . ." Tolman went on.

Lichteiman had found something, lower on the torso, a small amount of blood surrounding the vagina.

"What is this?"

"The bleeding from the chest wound must have run down toward her lap, before the victim collapsed to the left and struck the fetal position," Tolman suggested.

"Scalpel?" Lichteiman asked.

"Something very sharp. Probably surgical," the coroner confirmed. "Anybody can buy that stuff now."

"What time, doc?"

"Four, five hours ago. Enough time to come out of anesthesia at a hospital, rip off a chest bandage and want to die."

"Who is she?"

"Still checking. We've got Sinai and Midway looking into late surgeries."

"Who found her?"

"Some couple were at a party on Rodeo, were walking home to Benedict. Saw the white skin, thought it was a mannequin . . ."

"Check *this*," Lichteiman ordered.

"What?"

Lichteiman waved the coroner from the chest to the genital area.

"Can't tell rape, can't be sure until we get the body back to—"

"What are these marks?" Lichteiman asked, pointing to what seemed to be small welts, even blisters extending from the girl's red-blond hair to as far as the entrance to the vaginal lips.

The coroner called for another light, began to gauze a section, blotting the blood.

After a moment he sat back on his heels, shaking his head.

"What are they?"

"Jeezus Christ," the coroner said, "*teeth* marks."

"What?" Lt. Straub coughed.

"She didn't just have her tits cut off. She's chewed. Someone bit her, bit her . . . Jeezus Christ . . ."

"A fucking maniac," Tolman said. "We've got a fucking maniac."

Lichteiman stood up, looked at Straub, and headed back to his car. He felt his belt cutting into his stomach, thanks to a huge pizza he had devoured at Jacopo's just hours before. Pizza with onions and two Heinekens—then four Alka Seltzers. He slipped in behind the wheel of his car, opened his belt and loosened his shirt. He started to drive. He'd go up to Mulholland, catch a few hours sleep and get back down for the full report. With this second mutilation the pattern began to form, confirming that his talent would be used—a talent which in the beginning he believed would find little use, but which in the last seven years had had little rest. There had been the Hillside Strangler, the Silver Lake Strangler, the rapists at UCLA and USC. There were the isolated mutilations and decapitations at Covena and Riverside, and he was called out to Long Beach to help on the 1978 whore mutilations which, it turned out, were the work of an Italian sailor. The prostitute and hustler mutilations stemming from pickups on Sunset and Santa Monica Boulevard would have been enough to overload him on loan-outs to the LAPD. In a short time he had begun to notice the increasing horror in the home, the husband who would come home one evening and without a word wipe out himself and his family with a shotgun or poison. There had been the Kool Aid and the cults, the gurus and their women mowed down in Laurel Canyon. There were the sex crimes and the cocaine wars. But more and more, there were men hurting women.

OCTOBER 22

Marjorie had to tune out certain aspects of Carole Bender: Carole, forty-eight years old, a white-blonde with multiple face lifts, gushing, aggressive. Marjorie was attracted to her because she'd never met such an animated, articulate woman before. And Carole had sniffed her out, as if she were bird-dogging a new pal. As if auditioning, she had committed all the correct outrages at the Writers Guild party. Her eyes had linked into Marjorie's as if to say, *There's somebody important inside you. And I'm willing to take the time to find her.* . . . Of course, Marjorie had known a few of the mothers when the kids were in nursery school, one in particular being Joan Barron—but Joan lived in Bel Air and somehow they had never gotten around to mixing their families more than once or twice. Jack didn't really want to socialize, and Joan's kids, Jake and Jenny, were both slightly older than Danny and Courtney. Joan Barron had made contact, but not with the relentless energy of Carole.

Carole's assortment of small dogs ran around the living room, and a naked, dark young man named Nat was out behind the windows commuting between pool and Jacuzzi, sometimes stretching out voluptuously on a lounge.

"This is where you write?" Marjorie asked, looking over a paper-strewn living room complete with word processor.

"This is it."

They sipped some white wine. Carole told her about a screenplay she was working on. Then the focus moved onto Marjorie, and Carole didn't disappoint her: "To write anything decent you have to find out what tears really *mean*, Marjorie. I was raised in a Catholic school, and the nuns told me that God thought the most beautiful thing in the world was a child's tear. Sister Tomasino said, 'Yes, little Carole, if only you could shed a tear in confession. Oh, my what a wonderful gift for God.' *Well, that's tough shit*, I should have told her, because you see, Marjorie, I didn't *have* any sins. I was all of eight years old and I frankly did not have any sins. So I started to *make up* sins in the confession box. I told them I sassed a bag lady, and that I told a lie to a Woolworth salesman. I always tried to cry for the priest so that God would be happy. Your husband is your priest, isn't he, Marjorie?"

Marjorie leaned back into the soft cushions of an overstuffed sectional.

"My husband thinks I've made a good start. He wants me to succeed . . ."

"Hell-pecker, he does."

Carole was the only woman she had met in Beverly Hills who had New York strength, though that strength coexisted with her California zaniness. She lived in Trusdale, in a home worth over a million.

Carole claimed Trusdale was rather *declassé* and swarming with Arabs and Iranians, with Danny Thomas topping off the heap in his multi-acre Moorish palace. The entire front of Carole's home was covered with chips of what Jack always called Mussolini marble.

Carole was also the whitest woman Marjorie had ever seen. At any time of day she'd be wearing a completely white wardrobe, including big, schoolmarm-ish, white-rimmed glasses. Sometimes she wore very short white skirts, with tremendous white heels to lift her short body as high in the air as possible. She wore starlet-styled white hair, with a small wiglet to give still greater height and to hide a slight thinning spot on her crown. Marjorie had figured out that Carole's usual routine was to sleep until eleven, then get into a bath for at least two hours. Her face was flawless, thanks to several face lifts and eye bobs, except for her nose, which had a deep crevice just above the tip. Marjorie noticed that for highly public outings Carole filled the crevice with some sort of cosmetic paste which made the defect unnoticeable. She had heard from other women in town that Carole constantly gouged her own nose, that it was a psychological need which no one really understood, and no one discussed. Carole Bender's stark whiteness and self-abused nose were simply accepted givens. Only one person was said to have called her on either, and that was at a party many years before when a rather uncouth wife of a college coach got on line to bid farewell and thank Carole for hosting a marvelous, perfect dinner. After a stream of compliments, the coach's wife stared at her as though seeing her for the first time and asked quite loudly: "Hey, why are you so *white*?" Carole was said to have given her neither a reply nor a second invitation.

Carole had also been the one to take Marjorie on her first authentic Beverly Hills shopping trip. Marjorie had looked in all the obvious stores on her own, checked out the western counterparts of Gucci, Saks, and Ted Lapidus. Rodeo Drive also had Elizabeth Arden, Van Cleef and Arpels—and there was Cartier and Tiffany's—enough familiar names and goods to make Marjorie feel at home for window shopping. Carole led her to Devante's—"The Things that Dreams are Made of." They had lovely champlevé sets and magnificent wirework jewelry boxes. Carole showed her Georgette Klinger where she went for all her skin treatments—Gun Trigere Ltd. and Benelton Italian Knitwear and Black Willow mink from Jack Fenster. Sometimes Carole would march Marjorie right into Edwards-Lowell to try on a string of luxury furs and then march out, offended because nothing suited her. Their shopping trips were always fun—and while they usually bought nothing expensive, Marjorie could see Carole was memorizing every aspect of every material her eyes fell upon. She knew the ins and outs of buying and decorating as well as anyone. Carole had been unable to find a wallpaper she liked on one occasion, so she led Marjorie through the process of selecting a rose pattern from an antique print and having an artist lift it into reproduction onto a white fabric. Marjorie had never known anyone who pushed past the acres of available papers and fabrics to such levels of customized nerve. Carole also opened up the mysteries of Robertson and the Design Center. She laid bare the mechanics of antique buying. Wicker hunting became an art. She could spot a custom concept sofa and lay in wait for six months until just the moment when the showroom was about to send it back to its maker in San Francisco, then she'd swoop in and buy it for less than cost. Marjorie had actually been with her when Carole bought a six-thousand-dollar rattan set for seventeen hundred.

On this warm afternoon Marjorie pretended she didn't see Carole kiss her naked young man goodbye on his genitals as he lay still sunning near the pool.

"We'll be right back," Carole told him, and then marched Marjorie out to her Mercedes convertible. She had the top off for the afternoon, and made reservations for them at Ma Maison.

Over lunch Carole sensed Marjorie was still a bit gloomy, and had little trouble linking the gloom to Jack.

"You're lucky all you feel is tension in your marriage," Carole said. "Everybody I know who's still married is into open combat."

"Why?" Marjorie asked. "What's going on with everybody?"

"Why the battle of the sexes?" Carole laughed. "I think that battle has always been going on. Historically, a lot of it dates from the Victorian period when all this brainwashing went on. But the Jewish people have been busy creating problems too. Jews say there's got to be twelve good men to have a funeral. But where are they going to find twelve good men?"

Marjorie had to laugh.

"There aren't *any* good men," Carole went on, "but if you look at history as seen through the eyes of the female rather than the male, it's fascinating and it's very funny. I come from about the fourth generation of California women who have done their own thing in life."

"You do?"

"My grandmother divorced her Minister husband in 1899. After nine years of being beaten up, she divorced him, and she got it finalized in nine months, which was a record. He was an alcoholic, a Baptist

Minister in San José. She took all the kids away and brought them up herself by teaching music. Her own mother had to take over for a tubercular husband. That was a happy marriage in spirit, but he couldn't do anything because he was so weak. In my family all these strong women have supported the men. And my own father was a great believer in women. He admired his mother and grandmother, and he wanted me to be more or less the same, except that I had an older brother and we had very little money after the Depression. The whole trip was to educate my brother, send him to college. It was lucky there was anything left for me. What was Jack's father like?"

"According to Jack, he was completely under the influence of his old German mother—until Jack's mom came along, pried him loose, and encouraged him to become a cop—made a man out of him."

"Why the hell do people think the male is dominant?" Carole snorted. "I'll tell you why—because that's all you ever hear. As I said, four generations of my family knew damn well the woman was dominant."

"But what about the war between the sexes?" Marjorie wanted to know.

"I was at a party once where this man was saying women *liked* being raped. That's a terrible thing to say. It really is. But men have this fantasy that women like to be dominated."

"But when you think of things like sex organs, the differences in body shape, we *are* made to bear the children."

"Yes, but think of it this way: women extend the invitation, they say come on, sucker, come in and impregnate me like a flower. Women have been eternal, forceful con-merchants, but what has happened is that men have gotten into the media quicker. They have announced that they are the dominant force! And we say, oh fuck that, just lie back and enjoy it. Some say the hand that rocks the cradle rules the world. Or: behind every strong man there is a woman. But it's also true that women do not have this same craving that men have for greatness. This is what worries me about men. Why do they want it? Why do they want to get up there and say *I am the greatest,* while you and I can have a few laughs shopping on Rodeo Drive or watching a Morgan Fairchild flit from table to table?"

"A man seems to need bravura for plumage," Marjorie said.

"Fuck their bravura! Oh, I'd give anything to be twenty years younger," Carole admitted. "I really would because it is all adding up, you know. Twenty years ago I was tongue-tied, there was nowhere I could go, nothing I could say. Now I can go anywhere I want, say anything."

"It really is great."

"But it's a little too late for me. And don't think I'm not fucking mad about that. But that's a subject for another day."

She was home long before the school bus. She had pulled the car up to the garage, pressed the electronic control, and the garage door lifted open, rolling up into the ceiling like a black tongue. She got out and just made it back outside before the door automatically came down. She wanted to check if Tomás had watered the new lemon trees and the two torturosos they had stuck in to hide the water meter. She placed a finger in each pot and was happy to feel the soil was moist. Then she walked around to the front entrance. The mailbox was empty. Maria must have brought in the mail. Or maybe Jack had taken a break from his writing to read the mail and swim in the pool. She moved behind one of the white slabs of the entrance overhang.

Voices.

She turned and peered out from between the entrance monoliths. There were workers resting in the plastic surgeon's gazebo. A black, stretch limousine was in the driveway. A chauffeur was waiting. At the main entrance, half-cloaked by ficus trees, was a woman with a bandaged face and dark sunglasses. She looked fresh from the knife, her head lowered. The doctor, in shirt and tie, was tending to her. He put his arm around her, a professional comforting hug. The woman turned, hurried to the limousine, and climbed in. The chauffeur sealed the door and got in. The limousine backed out onto the street, floundered like a whale in the narrow harbor of the intersection, then pulled off. As Marjorie watched the car go, she felt the doctor's eyes shooting across, catching her. Dr. Huston was a large man, heavy, late thirties. A friendly smile and a wave. But he had caught her snooping.

Inside she approached the library, but heard Jack dictating. She retreated, deciding to change and hit a few balls on the tennis court.

At three-thirty, shouts and laughter. The children were home.

"Oh, imagine, a *red ribbon*. Student of the Week! I can't believe it. Oh, yes, Courtney, I'm sure you'll be Student of the Week soon, too." Then came the milk, 7Up, and cupcakes and licorice. Marjorie finally poured herself a cup of raspberry tea and sat down, watching her beautiful children devour their snack and move on to make a complete mess out of the den. They bring out the best in me, Marjorie thought, and the worst. Little Court who will be the great cheerleader, and then a famous actress. And Danny, who holds his own against electronic aliens, and climbs trees like a monkey, will be President. What wonderful little people.

During dinner Marjorie did her best to keep Jack cheerful. She knew a part of him was still at his mother's grave, still reliving the confrontations with Bernice. At one point she caught him staring at her. She wondered what he was seeing. Maybe he was thinking how young and attractive she had stayed? Or after seven years of marriage maybe he wanted someone younger and prettier. She worried.

Later she got all the signals they would make love again that night. He showered, flossed his teeth, and gargled. That always meant love. She herself had never been that calculated about preparations for romance, but he had trained her quickly and well. She showered after him, and by the time she went to the bed he was already lying naked, waiting.

Now might be the time to get through to him, before the lovemaking, she decided. After that he would go right to sleep.

"I thought we'd have a few of the neighbors over," she said, sitting on the edge of the bed.

"No, thanks."

"I thought we'd like to get to know them better. I think Mercer has poker games on Mondays. And the plastic surgeon. Aren't you curious about what he *does* over there?"

"Please, Marjorie . . ."

"I just think we should be more social. We need to mix more. We don't really have any friends here. Don't you miss having friends like we had in New York?" She leaned over him, began to move her hand over his chest, gently tickling his hair.

"No, I don't."

"Don't you wonder what goes on around here? Don't you want to find out what they're *doing* behind all that wrought iron and Carrara marble, and those electrified gates?"

"Marjorie, you should just relax. Plant roses or something."

He went to his closet and she listened to sounds which had taken on new meaning. She had never thought about his activities in his closet before, and the sniffing she had heard never signaled more to her than his usual post-nasal drip. Now she knew why he had also been reaching into his nightstand more frequently. Often she had been awakened by his *doing* things. She had thought he was rubbing his neck with Vicks or mixing an Alka Seltzer. At worst she had believed he might be using a dab of hydrocortisone cream for some itch. This night when he had put the lights out and climbed back into the bed she decided to get it out in the open.

"Are you using cocaine, Jack?"

"A little."

He rolled toward her, put his arms around her and began kissing her breasts. He would kiss her there and on the neck. Sometimes he kissed even her hair. But his lips rarely ever touched hers. *If you want to know if he loves you so, it's in his kiss* was how she remembered an old song.

She had never been able to use drugs herself. In fact, drugs were the main reason she had left teaching. She remembered the moment as though it was yesterday. Marjorie Krenner in front of her Applied English class, telling them how to prepare a job resumé when she noticed half the kids looked asleep. She told them she knew she was a little boring, but they had never dozed off in such large numbers before.

"We're high!" they had yelled out to her.

The kids even brought her samples. Then her friends seemed to have them, and finally drugs were in every singles bar. She tried grass a few times with Jack because he wanted to experiment and some of the couples they saw in New York flirted with the stuff. It was more like "Hey, let's make believe we're with it." Anything more than two puffs of marijuana made her feel ill. What she did finally understand were the sex-heightening powers of grass, and she had heard cocaine did the same. If only the kids in her classes and the FBI report had simply come right out and said "And also, human beings take drugs because it makes their sex wilder" it would have all made more sense.

She also knew most of the zanier, energetic stars in Hollywood and Beverly Hills were using cocaine on a regular basis. She had been particularly thrown when Belushi had died at the Chateau Marmont. They had seen him several times on the Strip, and once one of their neighbors had crossed telephone lines with his after a storm. Marjorie wasn't a dope. She knew most of the celebrities and people in the business who were running into trouble with the drug, were snorting huge amounts and usually moved into injections coupling rarefied cocaine with heroin. She had been at rock parties where the cocaine was passed around as though it were sugar at a tea.

Belushi had gone out to dinner with de Niro on Sunset Strip. Then there had been a show at the Improv, and a stop in at On the Rox. There he met a friend and they played until about one-thirty in the morning—Belushi dressed in jeans and wearing a bandanna tied on his head. Earlier that night he had ordered some drugs, and then his body was discovered the next morning in his hotel bungalow. A man under pressure. Needle marks on his arm. Excess. No limits in eating, drinking, or drugs. *From ethyl chloride to Quaaludes, he did every drug in the book,* Marjorie had read in the papers. "I wish I'd been there to protect him," one pal of Belushi's said after his body had been found. And Marjorie felt the same toward Jack. She *would* be there to protect him.

"I'm just using a little bit. No problem," he told her.

And she believed him.

He lay back now and she rose up, then lowered herself onto him. There were other ways, but this was the staple ecstasy of their union. From above she could control and he usually wanted her to reach orgasm first. Then he would relax and she could devote her full energies to teasing him. They never actually discussed it, but she knew his greatest erections would occur after an hour of teasing, in the final moments when he would take his arms from around her and place them outward on the bed, palms upward.

"I want you to try something," Jack whispered in her ear, moving her off.

"I don't want any cocaine, Jack."

"This is different."

"I don't want anything . . ."

"Just a little."

"I don't need anything, honey. You don't need it either . . ."

"It's just a little. You'll like this . . ."

He had moved his hand to the lips of her vagina and she could feel him touching her. It was enough to be in his warmth . . .

She so needed him she didn't want to speak anymore. She was falling beyond words just being next to him. She felt the energy of his body flowing into her. She didn't want anything to break the romance. When he sat up and reached to his nightstand she knew she would try to do what he wanted, but she wouldn't allow cocaine into her nostrils, not into her . . .

The garden night lights speckled the bedroom with shadows. She was aware of him unscrewing the top from a small vial, and she lifted her head to see him sprinkling some of the white powder onto her genitals. She half expected it to burn, started to protest, but his hand worked the powder over the lips of her vagina.

At first there was no unusual sensation. She watched him put some of the white powder onto his penis, smooth it over the corona. He lay back next to her, and she felt his fingers stroking the area of her clitoris. She reached down to take his organ and found him even fuller, larger. What the cocaine had done for him, or at least the *idea* of cocaine, was to make him harder than she had ever felt him. For a moment his fingers slipped, lost her tiny bud in the upper folds of the lips of her vagina. She was still waiting to feel any effect from the cocaine—but she felt only her own pleasure, full and satisfying as usual. It was fine. It was enough. She rose above him again, gently guiding him inside her, and she could feel her own moisture. Her nipples and breasts were accessible to his sucking and fondling, and she had almost lost all sense of time. . . .

The feeling.

The *new* feeling.

It started as a slight warmth, a growing female warmth beginning at the clitoris and moving to encompass the surface of her vagina. The warmth then began to wash down inside her, spreading out beyond the inner channel, finally beyond her womb to encompass her entire lower body. She felt her legs opening wider, actually felt the entire shape of his organ as she lifted herself up and slowly down until it reached deeper inside her than she had ever imagined possible. New sensations began to resonate through her, starting with what seemed to be a consciousness of each of her pubic hairs, then a new awareness of her contracting and releasing his member. It was as though her vagina had become some sort of muscular fist holding onto him. She felt the head of his penis rubbing against the recesses of her innermost tissues, pushing, touching, kissing her very insides. She was aware of a great unreality seizing her, of the cocaine heightening everything she had ever felt in sex. Then he sat up, with her still astride him. He was lifting her. He was lifting her into the air, and she began to hang onto him. She grabbed his neck with her arms, and her legs wrapped around his waist as he stood next to the bed.

Standing.

He was standing.

Click! Crunchhhh! For some reason she was hearing the sounds in her mind now. The sounds had been real, but now they were inside her head and she felt a fear creeping into the sexual pleasure. She thought she saw a shadow moving to her left, something darting behind a door. Then a black spot moved from the bottom of her right eye to the top of her eyelid. There was someone else in the room with them, someone watching their lovemaking.

No.

No one could be behind the door.

He was still inside her and he was standing and

then walking. He carried her, his hips thrust forward and she gripped him. He stayed in her, and she clamped onto him as though she would be lost if they separated. Now into the shadows of the hallway. To the stairs. Then down, down the stairs and out to the pool. She held onto him, swaying as he moved, his penis impaling her as though it were steel. She never even thought of speech, just a pleasurable moan, a purring. She was reduced to guttural sounds as he moved slowly into the heated water at the shallow end of the steaming kidney pool. He kept inside her as he sat on the steps. As he lay back she knew they were both in a greater ecstasy than they had ever known together. He began to suck on her breasts and reached down into the water to finger her clitoris with his one hand, and with the other he touched her anus. She herself began a rocking motion and she could feel it driving his penis still deeper inside her.

The *cocaine.*

This was the cocaine.

She felt guilt now, guilt for letting him put the drug on her. *I am losing control I am not in control the drug the drug it is not normal the children, the sleeping children, the maid, where is the maid . . .*

He was changing now. Moving. He came out of her and was standing. He took her hand, half-floated her into the Jacuzzi basin of the pool. He turned her toward him, had her sit down upon him again in the hottest waters of the whirlpool. His penis slipped easily back inside her and he had her lie back with her thighs over his and her legs wrapped around his waist. Once inside her he was free again to play with her breasts and lean forward to suck her nipples again. She lay back crying with happiness as she watched him devour her. She felt her groin fill, filling and hot and she pulling him into her still deeper. He settled into her, slowly turning, moving higher and higher above her.

Shadows moved at the edge of her vision. She twisted her head sharply to catch them, to see the intruder. They flashed again, and again, but she wasn't fast enough. The drug was causing black comets to fly across her retina, and yet she felt someone, something malevolent was with them. There was a third being somewhere *watching*.

The cocaine.

It was unreality. Unreality. *In me, in me, Jack come into me.* He made her lean back further, turned on the water jets and now the water bubbled and danced at her ears. Her legs were spread wider now over his kneeling thighs, raising her and exposing more of her clitoris, presenting it to the night and his manipulations. She began to cry with a confused joy, wanting to scream because her membranes were out of control. Her passage became personified, a separate being wanting him to run his penis harder against its walls. When she thought she could go no higher, he pressed himself between her legs with the force of a juggernaut, grasping her waist to keep the collisions solid, trembling. She found herself lifting her pelvis still higher to help his body rub more firmly against her clitoris as he moved in and out of her like some violent machine. He raised himself now in a kind of push-up over her upturned genitals, and he led her to drape her legs over his shoulders. Now he was pushing in and out of her and gazing into her eyes. The higher she raised her legs over his shoulders the deeper her body was penetrated by his terrifically swollen organ. As her first orgasm hit she wanted to scream but *the children, the children, Maria and the children and Miss Maggie . . .*

Jack's words:

I'm exploding, exploding I'm into you exploding, shooting and shooting.

She heard his voice growling at her ear and they fell into each other as though in a long, falling convulsion.

Later, knowing the cocaine secret, she became slightly nauseous and had to throw up.

CHAPTER SIX

NOVEMBER 1

The morning of Danny's birthday was crazy. Jack supervised the decorations in the backyard. He had Tomás hang up a huge "HAPPY BIRTHDAY DANNY" sign on the fattest eucalyptus tree in the backyard. He supervised the burst of crepe-paper streamers, red, black, and white, shooting off from the limbs to the house. He spent hours setting up and testing his color video camera with its RCA portable deck. He took some shots of the two Windsor children from up on Loonridge Hill. They were a few years older than Danny and Court, but they liked to come down to the intersection of Lost Orchard and Valley to play handball and on rare occasions use the Krenner's tennis court. Danny followed his father about, dressed in his first suit, hair shiny and combed, looking convincingly bewildered and secretly excited.

Jack couldn't wait to give Danny his Intellivision. There had always been a slight competition between Jack and Marjorie as to who actually presented the children with the gifts even though it was rather well known that Jack's money, or rather his charge cards were the means by which material goods, including toys, were purchased.

"Oh Daddy, I love Space Armada."

"Poker and Blackjack come with it, but I got you Astro Smash too, and *baseball*."

"Can we play, Daddy? Can we play?"

"Sure."

Jack hooked the game up to the large RCA television in Danny's room and he lay on the floor with his son reading the brochure and figuring out all the buttons and instructions. As usual, Jack didn't baby Danny when it came to competition, and even though Jack was able to win most of the games they ever played, Danny was slowly moving up on him. And with Intellivision, Danny seemed to be holding his own. Jack had a particularly hard time trying to compete with him on Space Battle. What seemed rather bewildering and complex to him seemed somewhat easier for Danny. He could press the control switches and have the blue, white, and yellow squadrons take off and return to base with some sense of authority and intelligence. Even after an hour of playing the game Jack hadn't quite mastered what "go to battle" meant, much less "the *radar* and *alien* screens."

"There is only one thing else I wish you had gotten me," Danny said.

"What's that?" Jack asked looking at Danny and the background of his room which included a microscope, a young erector set, a huge globe of the world, forty or fifty stuffed animals which had been relegated to the highest shelves for decoration more than use. There was a fleet of remote control cars, a Porsche, an Alpha Romeo, a Speak and Spell, electronic football, and a learning machine by Coleco. The room was a forest of expensive, intriguing, mindblowing toys.

"And what else did you want?"

"I don't know," Danny said. "But I bet there's something else."

Jack laughed, and gave his son a hug.

4:30 P.M.

Marjorie was rushing about gathering ferns and shrubbery leaves to garnish the buffet table when the man with the Moon Bounce arrived. He managed to lug the massive plastic sheeting into the backyard near the tennis court, and the inflation process began. Danny stood amazed, watching the form expand, with all the excitement of seeing a sleeping dragon awake.

Just after noon the elephant arrived in a huge long trailer-truck. The trainer, cowboylike, with a large straw hat obscuring his craggy, dark, young face, lugged planking into the yard to set up the boarding platform.

"I thought it was going to be a *baby* elephant!" Marjorie yelled.

"Look, lady, you just ordered an elephant."

The children were all from Danny's class at Douglas School. The parents had been invited to bring their kids and stay on for a drink. She hadn't gotten their names straight, nor their divorces, nor credits, but she hoped Jack would come out of himself to enjoy them.

"That's some elephant!"

Marjorie felt love and amazement for life itself as she watched the sweet, adorable children, lucky, coiffured children, gutsy children, arguing children, eating children. And when it was Court's turn on the elephant Marjorie was right up there with her.

Marjorie had invited most of the neighborhood to

stop by. Melissa Stark came down from her home at the top of Valley Road where it met Coldwater. She brought her infant girl, and Marjorie felt a rather special closeness to her. Melissa was a gentle, sweet black girl in her early thirties, who had been a secretary in Washington when she met her husband, a successful composer of movie scores. Melissa had come to Beverly Hills only a year before Marjorie, and Marjorie could see they had a lot in common. Melissa, like hordes of wives Marjorie had met, was trying very hard to be an actress.

6:15 P.M.

Carole Bender arrived late with her young boyfriend, just as the elephant and Moon Bounce were leaving and the party was beginning to settle into an adult cluster, while lingering children ran through the house playing with their favors. Carole was already high and she was still drinking.

"Personally," Carole told Dr. Huston, "I've discovered every emotion you'll experience in California can be traced directly to attacks by giant pollen from Arizona. How old are you, dear?" Her white rimmed glasses fell to the tip of her nose.

"You remember my husband, Jack?" Marjorie asked, leading Carole away from the doctor.

"Hello," Jack said.

"Oh, yeah, I remember *you*, honey," Carole shot at him, pulled loose from Marjorie's arm and walked right past him.

"Maybe you'd better have some food, Carole."

"Oh, Marjorie, I hope I'm not embarrassing you, am I? You know," Carole revved up her voice to take on the entire cluster of guests. "I'm actually convinced that God is going to punish us out here very soon. Did you know nobody in Beverly Hills goes to church?"

"That's because ninety percent of Beverly Hills is Jewish," Jack suddenly spoke up. Marjorie thought she was hearing things, that someone else had decided to bait Carole. But there Jack was, near the bar, his eyes locked on a slightly surprised Carole, her face whiter than ever.

"Bullshit," Carole dismissed him. "The Jews don't go anywhere either. Nobody does. Church in LA is going to Mann's Chinese, Knotts Berry Farm, or the La Brea Tar Pits. And all the schnorrers are driving around with bumper stickers that say 'Jesus is coming and boy will he be pissed.' You see, the way I've got it figured, God is going to cause this enormous— pardon the cliché—earthquake that will just knock all of California into the ocean. The only part I haven't figured out is whether the entire Mormon church is going to end up as stiff city for being the second largest corporation west of the Mississippi, or whether Donny and Marie are the only ones that are going to take the rap."

"They're pretty safe, aren't they?" Jack spoke up again. "They live in Utah, don't they?"

"They'll be taken during a Merv Griffin taping," Carole spat, and the rest of the guests simply looked from Carole to Jack as though watching a tennis match.

8:00 P.M.

Maria took charge of the remaining children playing Intellivision in Danny's room. Marjorie had invited a handful of acquaintances, including Jack's agent Gilda, to stay on for a light dinner, which was being prepared by a young caterer: raspberry ham, asparagus, and spinach salad. Carole quieted down and stayed in a corner with her boyfriend. As with most dinner parties Marjorie had attended in Beverly Hills, the conversation came around to real estate properties and a subtle snobbery about the uniqueness of their all living in the very special Beverly Hills. And when most of the homes were discussed it was because either Willy Shoemaker once owned this house, or Charles Bronson once lived in that house. Mercer had a little more to drink than usual, and was preparing a television movie in which he wanted to use Clark Gable's old ranch home in Encino, as well as film right at his crypt next to Carole Lombard's in Forest Lawn Cemetery, Glendale. He said he already was planning a documentary on all the countless places where the stars had left their imprints. He was busy clearing the rights to film at the old Montmartre Cafe which had once been the home of the Lee Strasberg Acting School and had discovered as sort of an extra bonus that the same building in the nineteen-twenties was a place where Rudolf Valentino danced with Pola Negri. Charlie Chaplin wooed Marion Davies on the same spot, and a young Bing Crosby did a little hoofing there as well. Marjorie had also noticed how the topic of death would often come up at smaller dinner parties, during or immediately following dessert. She had originally noticed the phenomenon on the few occasions she had dined with Jack's mother and sister. She came to the conclusion that when people were hungry they seemed to be more animated, more alive in their choice of subject matter. But once the human alimentary canal was satisfied, the minds of human beings turned philosophical. Mrs. Hutchins suggested that Mercer make certain to take his crew to the house where Marilyn

Monroe died in 1962. And she wondered why no one really filmed her grace site at Westwood Memorial Cemetery.

"Have you thought about shooting at the Grey-stone Mansion?" Gilda suggested. "Not only was it the home of the late oilman E.L. Doheny, but it was the scene of murder and suicide in 1929. I'm not sure exactly who killed who." And from that point the guests began recalling the necrology of Beverly Hills with addresses such as 9820 Easton Drive, where Jean Harlow's husband Paul Bern fatally shot himself in the head. That same house was later purchased by Jay Sebring, who was killed in the Sharon Tate murders in 1969.

"You should do a documentary on the curse of Hollywood," Carole Bender suggested while publicly applying a fresh layer of whiteness to her face. "Make sure you don't miss any of the suicides or murders. You know, do Jack Cassidy, and Pier Angeli, and Janis Joplin, and Sal Mineo, Freddie Prinze, Lana Turner's Stompanato, Robert Walker, Bugsy Segal. Christ, you might as well put in Bobby Kennedy as well. They shot him down at that hotel."

It wasn't until after dinner that Marjorie noticed the strange body language evolving between Carole and Jack. Carole had quietly begun to speak to almost everyone in depth, but steered clear of Jack. She waited until after the others had brandy before she called down the length of the table to her host: "Are you working for Niko Aris?"

Jack had been deep in conversation with Gilda when he heard Carole's voice. "Yes," he said, waiting.

"He's very *unclean*, don't you find?" Carole slurred, still holding onto a plate of spinach salad.

All the other conversation at the table stopped. Marjorie noticed the guests deliberately sipping drinks, turning their snifters of brandy.

Carole sighed, "I wrote a script two years ago, when Niko was dating that Indian prince. They used to gamble in Monte Carlo for three days straight, then devour a dozen lobsters right at their blackjack table. Niko was always skinny as a rail, and yet he'd get up every morning, breakfast, brunch, lunch, tea, dine, sup, and suck!" She grinned sweetly at Jack and the guests, then sipped her glass of wine.

"Great wealth causes great envy," Gilda said slowly, protectively.

"Don't make me laugh," Carole said softly, but switching a tone-gear from disagreement to argument. "I'm sure Jack hangs around his house. It's a stinkhouse, you know, dead flies on the window sills, come spots on the peg wood floors. He's the only faggot I know who has a dirty mansion."

"I do business with Niko," Jack underlined. "I'm not interested in his sex life."

"Well, let me tell you what his sex life is," Carole laughed, "*Greekie parties.* That's what he has. He invites two hundred of his Greek faggot friends to come over the night before he gives a real party, and the faggots sample the chili and garlic bread around his pool and they kind of just pray someone like Joan Collins shows up. And then the next night, after the dry run, so to speak, that's when Niko has the stellar putzes over. They come to his mansion, eat the skinny fags' leftovers, and get stains on their Gucci pants."

Marjorie got up from the table, moved to Carole's side. "Carole, would you help me with the coffee?"

"Oh, coffee my ass!" she blurted, stuffing a last forkful of spinach salad into her mouth.

11:00 P.M.

"Why did you invite Carole?" Jack asked when he and Marjorie were finally in bed.

"I didn't know she got like that when she was drunk. She certainly livens things up—but I'm sorry. She was horrible. I also heard her put Gilda in her place."

"Gilda doesn't need to be put in her place. Her place is pretty important, and I'd like to keep her as my agent. You ought to earn the money she does!"

Marjorie thought that over a moment.

"Jack, I know you have to play the game with a lot of these movie people, but you don't have to worship them. Most of these people are the opposite of everything we ever believed in."

"It costs us fourteen thousand bucks to open our doors here every month, Marjorie."

"And I'm sorry I'm not earning anything yet. I'm trying as hard as I can. I think my book will be good."

She heard his silence, and for a moment the preposterousness of her enthusiasm struck even her. Even if her book was quite good it would at best lead only to a few thousand, certainly not enough to ever pay one month's mortgage. In her silence she suddenly felt quite useless.

She watched him get out of bed, go into his closet. She knew what he was doing. He came back to bed, used a spray antihistamine, and put the lights out. Then his hand reached over and took hers. He moved closer, held her, but there was something different. It was a long embrace; he seemed to be clinging to her with a need beyond sexuality. Finally he rose on top of her but the residue of despair had slowed the flow of lubricants in her body. He didn't mention cocaine, but put saliva on his hand, slicked his phallus, and came into her with a sudden thrust. She felt what was happening was not quite loving, but decided not to mention it. She felt he was straining his body, pushing himself—and when he was finished, he rolled off exhausted and—she thought—fell asleep.

MIDNIGHT

Jack knew he had taken too many thick lines of coke to drift into any space as lovely as sleep. He lay with his back to Marjorie, relieved that he wouldn't have to attempt conversation. He felt as though he were only a grain or two from needing to leap out of the bed and hang his head out the window to let the cool night air relieve his creeping chemical anxiety. He lay perfectly still, performing a breathing rhythm that would signal sleep. And it was only a few minutes later that he knew Marjorie was in dream land.

He tested her sleep by sitting up slowly and then standing next to the bed.

No change in her breathing.

For a moment he was afraid he would let out a shriek, that he would run to the bedroom phone and scream for help. He would do what one neighbor had told him. If you *really* are in trouble call the fire department and tell them your house is burning down. He could see the scene in his mind. The phone at his ear. "Fire department! Help! My house is burning down. The flames are getting hotter! Help me because the police take too long to come." Perhaps he should switch from the cocaine to amphetamines. But for some reason he thought amphetamines just then would give him a heart attack. Cocaine merely gave him the speed needed for his time. If he could wait until the overdose had been slightly consumed he would level out and enjoy a tremendous sense of well being. But the coke was less dependable now than in the beginning. He was taking doses dangerously close to dissolving whole sections of tissue in his nose, and already he had experiences of bugs under the skin. Something biting him in his elbow, now behind his neck. *There,* by his knee and his thigh. Something crawling near a testicle. Fleeting phantom bugs trying to gnaw their way from beneath his skin.

He moved barefoot to his closet, put on a robe and slipped a small vial and spoon into a pocket. He stepped into the outer hall and found himself beginning to check the window locks, running his fingers along the drafts of the sills. After several minutes, or was it seconds, he felt his anxiety accelerate, explode into a pervasive depression. The depression fell upon him like a fog from the night, mummifying him, wrapping about him tightly, trapping the bugs inside his very organs.

He thought this would be death forever. The final assault in the darkness that would make his aorta explode. He moved to the center of the largest picture window of the upper hall. Through it, in the light and shadows of the backyard, he saw the animals looking at him. He wondered why so many animals would be in his backyard staring at him—hundreds of wolves, thousands of coyotes, a rear yard made entirely of snarling, hairy animals.

He knew they were only shadows. But the sounds of a coyote kill high in the canyon were real. Yapping. The yapping sounded like that of a dozen puppies playing with a toy. The coyotes were coming closer into the streets now, nearer to his house. Every night it seemed they killed someone's cat or dog. The summer must have swelled their population beyond the two thousand said to live within the boundaries of Beverly Hills.

Now he found himself in Danny's room. On top of the television sat an antique night-light, softly illuminating a painted glass scene of a mountain and lake. In the meager glow he saw Danny had kicked off his blanket with the race car designs, and he used it as an excuse to kiss his son as he covered him gently, tucking him in. For several minutes, he sat on the edge of the car bed holding his son's hand. But the fear of a heart attack returned to him. He needed to busy himself, pull his mind away from the cocaine. He stretched out on the floor, turned on the television and switched to the Intellivision hookup. The space battle module was in place. A touch of the reset button and the pulsing electronic beep began to draw him. On the screen the half dozen enemies began their beeping advance from the outer recesses of the screen. In the middle was his home base, and he released all his squadrons to halt the approaching invaders. Another voice began to speak from deep inside his brain. He felt as though there were a little mouth in his hypothalamus. A little mouth with little lips saying, "I can't take much more. I'm terrified."

I don't want to do it.

But I'm going to do it.

For a moment, the picture of his mother's gravestone flashed across his mind. His mother buried beside her father at Woodland Cemetery. "Oh really now, Jack, you haven't grown up yet. There's much too much pressure. You're really not worthy of the Mercers or Dr. Huston. You're socially inferior and you haven't got the money to play the game. Jack, you're the only one on the block without a Mercedes. They all know what the Seville means, regardless of how many telephones and monitoring devices you care to install."

Now he was flying right through his eye sockets across the room and into the television set. He was in with all the sparks and electronic beeping. He was there on the mother ship with the alien squadrons heading for him. His blue, white, and gold counter squadrons were sailing forth, getting closer to the first infestation. *But, oh my God, how am I going to pay the mortgage? How can I pay an $8,500 mortgage every month? How can I send my kids to Douglas school for $6,000 a year? How can I pay $200 a week for food? How can I employ two servants for more than $1,000 a month? How can I repair the house? Pay for the new roof? Fix the carpeting? Buy the drapes? Clothe my wife? Pay her allowance? Feed the animals? How can I keep earning $15,000 a month and breathe? How can I keep my family alive?*

1:00 A.M.

Sounds. She heard the sounds again. Jack was gone from the bed.

This time they were clearly *kitchen* sounds amplified on the intercom. She reached up and turned down the volume. She remembered her exhaustion, the party; she saw it was still the middle of the night, and was about to go back to sleep. Their *sex*, there was something about their sex that still nagged at her. She got out of bed, walked to the bedroom windows. She could see shadows moving within the sunroom. Someone or something was prowling in the house. But Sandy and Sam were silent. It had to be Jack.

Her throat reminded her how dry she was. She would go down and have a drink with Jack. It was too late for juice. *Perhaps tea.* She moved barefoot along the carpeted hall and down the center staircase. As she started through the den, she could see Jack eerily silhouetted through the double set of sliding glass doors where the kitchen L shot off from the main house. He seemed to be lingering, his back to her, facing into the open refrigerator. She knew he couldn't hear her approach. She thought about humming, making some sound so as not to startle him. And yet another part of her made her step even more quietly. Her intelligence had not realized what was going on, but her senses ordered an alert. She felt adrenaline leaking into her blood and only a faint warning flashed into her brain—a signal that she was, in some way, in danger.

At the entrance to the kitchen, she saw Jack was wedged between the open refrigerator door and the shelving.

She heard a tearing in her mind, as her mental computer kicked up the memory of foul milk, the ghastly odor of death. Still somehow she was moving forward like a performer in a play and she found herself saying *Hi*, at the same time something inside her wanted to scream.

Jack did not jump at her sound. He turned toward her. She saw his eyes, his face pathetic and glazed and drugged.

What is that in his hand? What is that . . .

Her mind froze.

He was holding a container of milk. *He's holding the family milk between his legs, his penis hanging into the plastic mouth of the family milk. Oh God oh God . . .*

Gushingly he continued to urinate into the container.

"Oh, my God!" Marjorie hurrying to her husband,

taking the milk container from his pathetic hands. She saw tears in his eyes as she set the container down, and then reached her hands around him. She embraced him, crying "Oh, God, oh my poor husband oh God Jack . . ."

"I'm sorry," he said. "I'm sick . . . I'm very sick . . ."

PART II

CHAPTER SEVEN

NOVEMBER 2
2:00 A.M.

Somehow she had managed to get him into the bath.
"This will help you, Jack. You will feel better." A snake
of fear crawled deeply inside of her, moving from her
stomach up toward her heart and filling her with a
bloated fright. Somehow she had taken the milk carton from him, put her arms around him, and closed
the refrigerator door. Her mind was fighting to re-
press it, a nightmare. *Bury it. Yes, bury it.*

As she moved him she was aware of a tremendous
yapping from somewhere on the upper canyon slope.
She'd pretend it was only a kennel. Yap! Yap! Yap!
Cute little dogs, a kennel. *Someone has a kennel. One
day she would walk up to the end of the street, meet the
neighbors on the higher ridge and find the kennel. It
isn't a pack of coyotes. There are no coyotes. No coyotes
up there ripping a rabbit or someone's pet apart . . .*

She knelt beside the tub and soaked his back.
She'd keep contact, a tactile link at all times. He
didn't look at her. His eyes froze to the left and downward as though staring into the marble shadows of
the cavernously luxurious tub. Her husband so beautiful. She had never seen him so lost; yet even in this
lostness he was dazzling. At this point of exploding
confusion she felt like falling into his full and shining

lips. *Oh yes your husband has such gorgeous bedroom eyes dark eyebrows lucky lucky woman you Marjorie his beautiful dark hair that breaks and falls naturally in stunning masculinity . . .*

"What's wrong with me, Marjorie?"

Her full grown man in the tub, knees up against his chest, soap suds like a soft porn movie.

"You're under pressure . . ." She must think. She must do better than that. Nerves, the snake at her throat now.

"Am I losing my mind? I'm drifting, Marjorie. I'm being wrapped in cellophane."

She helped dry him off; a child. The towel, its innocent art of animals peering out from great jungle leaves; her husband, her well-behaved child as she dried his legs, and arms and genitals. (*Hurry, Mommy, it's cold. I want to stay in the pool. Can we get another plastic swan?*) She put his Superdad nightshirt on, helped him into bed. The night was cool. She'd leave the windows open. A lot of fresh air, the electric blanket on low. He'd be comfortable. In the morning she'd know what to do.

Click!

Clunk!

The memory of sounds. Now she knew what most of the sounds had been.

9:30 A.M.

"Court?" Danny said, grabbing the glue from the garden room table, and pulling his chair closer so Maria couldn't possibly hear from the kitchen. "What's the worst accident you ever saw?"

"I don't know," Courtney said. "Why do you want to know?"

Danny began to insert his scissor into the rubber

cap of the mucilage bottle. "I just thought Daddy had an accident last night."

"You don't go to doctors just for accidents. You go for checkups to make sure your heart is working."

The two things Danny remembered about the night before was his run of luck playing five-card stud on the Intellivision against Courtney and the sound of someone crying in the middle of the night. But as the hours of morning passed, he even forgot about those events. And now he was curious about where Mommy had taken Daddy, and whether he could cut out more paper dolls than Courtney or Maria. Finally, before noon, he was thankful Maria had stopped playing with them and had gone back to scrubbing the kitchen floor. He knew his Mommy always wanted someone to play with them, teaching them, and he appreciated it. But it was really very hard to talk about secrets if somebody was always around saying, "Hey, let's go play catch," or "Do you want to plant a cactus?"

"You know I was just thinking that maybe we better ask Daddy to build us a tree house," Danny said.

"You got the mud house. We need a swing. Tell him we need a swing. We don't even have a swing."

Danny took the Magic Marker he wanted and began to smudge in a spectral decaying mouth with one eye larger than the other. Danny used the pen to put the finishing touches on a few snaggle teeth. "Maybe we can make the tree house on our own. We could take like a pole and tie a rock on the end of it and a string and throw it up and then tie the string to the end of a rope and pull the rope up . . ."

"What do you want to put in the tree house?" Courtney wanted to know.

"Oh maybe a table."

"What else?"

"A chair."

"I'd like my tea set."

"Yeah. But we should also have some stuff for protection."

"What do we need protection for?"

"Just in case," Danny explained. "In case somebody tried to climb up when we were up there and we didn't want them climbing up. That's why I think we could use some cement up there. See, if a robber comes we just throw all of it down on him. It goes *bang* on his back. That's what we'd do. *Thud, bang* on his back."

"I wish Mommy would buy us a white mouse."

"I want a kangaroo rat." Danny thought that over a moment. "But first the tree house. First we need a tree house. If we both ask Daddy, he'll give it to us."

10:20 A.M.

The young Thai boys were kind, smiling as they took the car at the Wilshire Medical Building. She held Jack's hand and waited for the elevator, hoping to make it safely inside before any other human beings appeared, but a young man got in, bringing what had to be his mother. Then an older lady with an aluminum walker and two other patients with escorts entered before the elevator doors finally shut. The metal box took them up, stopping at every floor, and Marjorie watched Jack's face, knew he was suffering terribly. She hugged him, held on to him, trying to keep some connection. At last they reached the fifth floor. She led him quickly down the hall to Dr. Bernstein's office.

The waiting room was empty.

Marilyn, the receptionist, was on the phone behind the partition discussing payments, charges. Marjorie signaled her to make their presence known, then she and Jack sat across from a large Chagall print of angels bearing Christ aloft. Another painting, abstract, some sort of pastel sprayed with a lacquer.

11:00 A.M.

An oriental assistant began the routine tests; Jack signed the informed-consent slip required for the treadmill test.

"I don't think he needs a *treadmill* test," Marjorie protested.

"The doctor ordered it. You'd be surprised what shows up under stress."

Oh, no I wouldn't, Marjorie felt ready to snap back, but she knew her nerves were rather frayed. She'd keep calm and sensible, understand everything she was told. She had to understand, for Jack's sake, for herself, for Danny and Courtney. And in a moment she was close to tears. She moved quickly to the window of the examination room. Pushing the garish, geometric-design drapes aside, she stared down at a parking lot.

The nurse wanted samples of blood, urine, and feces.

"What will you look for in the blood?" Marjorie asked.

Jack was laughing with the nurse, exchanging double entendres, flirting a little over the clattering test tubes. At least he was coming out of his daze, Marjorie thought. She was still trapped in hers.

Barechested, Jack lay on a leather examination table. The nurse spot-shaved him and planted electrodes.

Marjorie knew it was not in the chest, not in the veins or arteries. Whatever was wrong with Jack, it would not be found or cured in the body. She wanted to see Dr. Bernstein, competent, highly recommended Dr. Bernstein, who treated celebrities and who could make Jack well.

11:25 A.M.

Marjorie alone with the nurse. "Do you get any men in here who abuse their wives?" Why was she asking that? She wanted to pull the question back.

"God, yes," the nurse admitted, shuffling through a pile of Blue Cross billing applications. "We had a doctor who used to bring his wife in here. She was sixty-eight and he was seventy-two, I think. Sometimes the poor wife could hardly walk. He'd hit her and push her down the steps. She had Hodgkin's disease on top of it."

"Oh, no. What'd she do about it?"

"She'd cry."

"Couldn't she report him?"

"No, she was too old. When women are too old, you know, they don't want to start all over again. When he'd bring her into the office here, he'd treat her real sweet and kind."

"He'd help her get medical help after *beating* her?"

"Oh, yes, that was it. Terrible. We all knew what he was doing, but nobody could say anything, except Dr. Bernstein. He used to say something."

"What do you think would motivate a husband to try to . . . injure his family?"

"I think it's usually something the husband thinks the wife did to him a long time ago. And he never forgave her for it. A secret lover or something, another man."

Marjorie got the gown ready while Jack completely undressed after the treadmill. She helped him into the blue paper gown with white trim around the lapel and translucent plastic ribbons that fastened in front. Alone in the room with her now, she saw his public energy disappear. Without saying a word, they knew they had both been performing. It didn't make the matter go away. It was still there and had to be dealt with. She helped him back onto the examining table, pushed a stool below for his feet. He sat there like a huge doll. A life-sized male doll. And she embraced him while his eyes stared at the wall.

Again she left him alone, moved out to the technician in the laboratory alcove. The technician looked up, smiled from behind two centrifuges and chromography equipment. Marjorie stuttered, finally began to form the words, "Can blood ever help diagnose mental disease?"

"Oh yes," the technician said. "There's a couple of blood tests that psychiatrists always order."

NOON

Dr. Bernstein made his exuberant entrance, not much taller than a dwarf, he radiated kindliness. This distinguished penguin, Marjorie thought, wanting to assault him with gratitude, *thank you thank you oh God thank you we are so alone out here we don't have anyone to tell thank you my good doctor thank you.* Then a delay, an emergency EKG for a seventeen-year-old girl. A possible heart attack. Marjorie watched her rushed in, glimpsed her hooked to a bleating machine. She was frightened for her. Somewhere inside her came a small prayer for the stranger.

False alarm. The girl was okay.

Now the doctor was finally in with Jack.

"Have you been to see any doctors this year?"

"No," Jack said quietly.

"Good, that means you've been healthy. Any headaches?"

"No."

"Any problems like a little nasal headache or something?"

"Sometimes I feel like I have emphysema."

"I don't like the term emphysema. I mean, sometimes you feel congested, or it's hard to breathe, but we all feel like that in Beverly Hills."

"Right," Jack agreed.

"Any blood in the stools?"

"No."

"How often do you have to urinate at nighttime? After you've gone to bed?"

The nurse and technician came to move him in for the treadmill. Dr. Bernstein signaled Marjorie to stay behind, that he wanted to talk to her alone. He closed the door.

"What's it all about, Marjorie?" he asked.

Marjorie sucked in air, began to speak rapidly, guiltily delivering privileged private information: "We're very happy. You know we have two beautiful children. He's under great pressure. We owe a lot of money. He thinks they want to get rid of him on a picture. You know our lovely kids, Danny and Courtney. Oh my God, Doctor, I found him urinating in the milk in the middle of the night."

"Into what?" Dr. Bernstein inquired, unamazed; he just hadn't heard her.

A beat.

"I saw him pissing into the family milk."

Another beat.

"He admits he's ill and needs help," she continued. "We only know you in town, the only doctor. I knew he'd need a physical first. Why would any man urinate in the family milk?"

Dr. Bernstein sat down on a small aluminum chair. His voice was low, matter of fact. "What you're really telling me is that he's producing a difference in his normal character."

"That's for sure."

"After the tests today, we have to first look at his brain to rule out the possibility of any mass in the head itself as a cause for a change in his normal behavior. The first thing we'll jump to as soon as we get the normal routine out of the way is a CTG scan. We'll get a computerization of the brain, looking for—"

"A tumor?"

"Yes, we wouldn't expect a psychiatric problem."

"*Urinating in the family milk?*" Marjorie repeated the offense.

"This is a change in the personality, and for that we look into the brain. We had a situation here last week, not quite that way, but this patient who is known to have heart disease and diabetes was invited to a party. She went to the party in a dirty nightgown. Now that was a change from what we'd expect of her. As it turned out, she didn't have a tumor, but we had a different problem. We brought in the specialists—the neurosurgeons and neurologists—and they went over everything, and they said there was no tumor. So they moved on then to what could be causing an effect *like* a mass in the brain; that meant looking at the arterial system. What *is* irritating the brain? This patient had a headache, a severe headache. We did the arteriogram looking for an aneurism formation because that could create the same irritation as a brain tumor. We found, finally, one of her ovaries had become diseased, and it was throwing off a poison which irritated the brain in the same way as a tumor."

"And what if all had proved normal?"

"If all those proved normal, then we'd have really been up a creek, because it didn't fit into a proper psychiatric syndrome."

"Doctor, my husband has been *peeing* into our milk! He's putting poisons into—"

"Urine is not a poison," Dr. Bernstein cut her off.

"What?"

"Urine is a waste, not a poison. You wouldn't normally want to put it into your mouth, but you could drink all the urine in the world and not die. When a person is in the desert, and he can't find any water he can survive by drinking his own urine."

Marjorie couldn't speak. When the words finally came out, they were too loud. She was screaming. She was screaming at poor Dr. Bernstein: "You make it sound like he was planning a treat for us! *He was pissing in our milk, Doctor! You don't piss in anyone's milk unless you hate them! We're not in a desert, we're in Beverly Hills, for Christ's sake!"*

Dr. Bernstein reached over, took Marjorie's hand. Finally she was back in control.

"There are a lot of men who feel they hate their families, Marjorie. There seem to be more and more men who come in here worried about feelings they have. They describe wanting to reach out and slap their wives or their children. They talk about passing them in the hall, or sitting with them at dinner and having the urge to reach out and hurt them. Plunge a fork into them, a knife, sock them. We're living in a time where men and women do not particularly like each other. A lot of men complain that their wives want careers they are not even remotely suited for. I have one ex-starlet wife who can barely speak English, who goes around applying only for executive positions. In front of guests the husband may ask if the wife could serve a little more lamb, and the wife tells him to get up and get it. They're competing, Marjorie. Men and women are competing. Husband and wife, lovers—competing. Do you understand? I have a problem in my own family now. My son and daughter-in-law are getting a divorce, a beautiful gal. But what happened is, after getting married, after five or six years, sometimes it's seven, sometimes it's nine or ten, the husband is moving up in his career, and the wife still wants to remain at the same level. A separation of the pathways is what I see here for my son. They've got children, *my* grandchildren, and it's all falling apart. Louise, his wife, just wants to be a homebody and love her children and husband, cook for them, clean the house for them. But Bert, my son, he's not interested in that anymore. He loves his family, but they're not keeping up with him, and he's going to leave them behind. A wise woman will always try to keep up with her husband. I think the wives who are fighting to stay close to their husbands, to keep up with them, are the wiser. Like you, Marjorie. You mustn't feel any guilt about your attempts at a career. If you had slowed down, Jack would have left you behind anyway. What's going on with him has nothing to do with your ambition, because you're smart. You'll always make certain your husband is number one, that you're number *two*, and a fairly close clever number two. But if you got to be number one, your husband would say, 'To hell with this, I want no part of it.' That would be a pressure on him."

"Maybe I'm in between," Marjorie said softly.

"We're *all* in between," Dr. Bernstein comforted.

"There's a lot that's up for grabs. My own wife would like to be Eva Peron if I let her. But when I'm working in one area, and she tries to move in, I say, 'Forget it, honey. You go work someplace else while I'm in this spot.'"

Dr. Bernstein stood. "Once we rule out the organic side," he said, "then we can move onto the psychiatric."

"If he has to go to a psychiatrist, would it have to be right here in Beverly Hills? What would you advise?" Marjorie asked.

"Here in Beverly Hills no one will know your husband is going to a psychiatrist unless you or your husband tell them."

"The shrinks don't *talk* here?"

"If they talked, I wouldn't have any part of them. This chart in my hand is your husband's history. If you didn't come in here jointly, I wouldn't make this information available to you. The patient has a right to privacy. His illnesses are protected information. You're working as a team to help your husband and that's different, but if your husband were to tell me, don't tell my wife about this or that, I'd have to respect his wishes unless it was something drastic."

"I understand," Marjorie said.

CHAPTER EIGHT

NOVEMBER 14
7:45 P.M.

Jack sat in the den with Danny watching *The Incredible Hulk* on the Advent. He was sprawled on one end of the sofa with his feet shooting out over the matching ottoman. It was a special time of the evening, with Danny and his Daddy watching TV while Marjorie gave Court her bath, and the maid cleaned up the dinner dishes in the kitchen. Jack loved the way Danny would begin to rattle his legs whenever a scary part came. Marjorie had given them their favorite chocolate pudding, and there were hard candies for Courtney and a licorice pipe for Danny. But at some level in Jack's brain there was a low boiling and he knew he was now only waiting for it to get dark.

He could see Marjorie was happy, hopeful now that he was seeing Doctor Dorin. Oh, yes, a wonderful, brilliant psychoanalyst. And on *one* level he himself enjoyed the opportunities to talk about himself, to begin the confession which he knew had to come.

At the very first session Jack had burst into tears. He had driven to Dr. Dorin's office on Ventura Boulevard—a safe distance from Beverly Hills. His confession would not be heard over the hill. Not even a whisper would reach Beverly Hills. Dr. Dorin sat in a plush leather chair with a small side table holding his pad and pencil. How dare he—a pad and pencil! Dr. Dorin, forty-five years old, medium height, nonathletic, cherubic from good dinners and a nice Sherman Oaks life, his boring suit, nice tie, pleasant voice, and a smile.

At the start of the session, Jack spoke quietly, but swiftly, he would tell everything he could. No, he was not very happy. No, he did not like his neighborhood. He had no close friends in California. No, he wasn't making enough money. Yes, the mortgage was an extraordinary contract to drive him insane and there was no way he could keep up eighty-five hundred a month. No, he didn't share the economic pressures with Marjorie, not the specific ones. Only lately she had found out because charge cards were being cancelled.

The questions he remembered:

Don't you know any of your strengths and weaknesses, Jack? Don't you know what you believe in? Do you think your past controls you? Don't you know how you got where you are? Don't you know you're indulging in guilt and shame? Don't you look inside yourself for the causes? Do you always think everyone is putting you down? Did you ever think about not tolerating people, jobs, or situations that are downers? Don't you ever relax, or meditate, or listen to yourself? Don't you have any hobbies? Don't you practice being a social animal? Don't you know you are not just an object to which bad things just happen? Don't you know that you can change your life?

And his answers: *I don't seem to know what I'm really thinking anymore. I know that I have a great deal of fear. I know since my mother died, an old horror of death sits on me. I know that I wake up in a cold sweat two, three times every night. I know I have some powerful sex need. I know I'm taking cocaine, and before that*

*I took Valium, and before that I smoke and drank. I
know that I'm hiding somebody underneath me, inside
me. I know I'm afraid of my feelings, afraid of the anger
and rage that I know is inside of me. I know that there is
a very ugly part in me. An ugly little child that if I ever
really faced I would die. I know I take drugs to keep the
ugly person quiet, the ugly part of me. I know that I need
to drug myself. I know I am beating myself over the head
with a metal plate and cutting myself with a razor just
slice by slice, and that the blood is running swifter. I
know that my compulsion has been continuing longer
and longer after my drugs have worn off.*

"What is so frightening?" Dr. Dorin asked.

"The pain," Jack had said. "There is a spiraling
pain inside of me that is out of control."

"Can you give this pain some type of name? Can
you tell me anything specific about this pain?"

Jack began to move his lips but no sound came
out.

"I can't hear you," Dr. Dorin said.

"I don't believe . . . in life anymore," Jack said,
and then covered his face so the doctor wouldn't have
to watch him cry.

After the first week of sessions, walks and reaching out to other human beings were part of the doctor's orders. The actual physical act of walking
counteracts depression, he was told. And Jack had
made a solid attempt at a friendship. He called up Dr.
Huston, the plastic surgeon across the street. Gerry
Huston had even invited him over, given him a tour of
the brick home and office; there was the Barker
Brothers living room furniture, the excessive use of
wood paneling. And most impressively, the shiny
stainless steel operating room. Then the dreadful

small talk: "Oh yes, Gerry, so you went to Bel Air High? Oh, I see, Gerry, so your story is really one of a rise to riches. You've got that strong peasant spirit like the rest of the stars. Oh yes, we see the bandaged ladies leaving, getting into their limousines. All of those shiny, sharp instruments, hundreds, cases full of them. And an autoclave, sterilization procedures. Of course, Gerry, take the phone call, I'll just wait here. I was premed for three years myself until I found out I was color blind and couldn't see the titration end points."

NOVEMBER 16
8:00 P.M.

"I'm going down to the gym for a workout before it closes," Jack called to Marjorie.

"It will do you good, honey," Marjorie agreed.

From the upper hall Jack could go straight down the servant stairs to the garage without having to pass Marjorie again. The press of a button. The automatic door began its chain-rattling lift and the two-minute automatic light came on. He went to a set of file cabinets he kept in the garage; on top, in plain view, was his gym satchel, a harmless blue and white bag with his equipment. He backed the Seville out and pressed the Genie control. The garage door closed.

He backed further out of the driveway, shifted into drive, began the sweep around and the climb up out of Valley Road. The headlights flashed against the walls and gates, and gave the streets an almost maritime look; the houses were like festive, great, illuminated yachts clinging to the dark quay of the road.

Midway up the block, the richest neighbors had long ago put up Bastille-size walls. At one mansion, Chicanos were working late, dark men carrying pieces of dead trees, bearing them to the inside of their dilapidated truck. Warning bumps had been constructed every hundred yards or so to slow vehicles in case of children at play, as if any children could possibly escape the walls. In the final curves, the lights of the Seville flickered on a row of straight monstrous cypress trees. These trees he remembered from Italian cemeteries, trees for the dead. Then he was rolling down Coldwater.

As he drove he recalled his last session with Dr. Dorin:

"You see, doctor, I can solve the literary problems. I'm good at story and script, but I'm not very good with my life. If I'm writing something, well, a first draft, I seem to always be missing a level of compassion. But then I can always go back and in the second draft put that in. Research it if I have to. I can't do that with my own life. I'm not compassionate in my first actions. Does that make sense to you? There is something that stops me from opening up to the warmth of another human being. Can you understand that, Doctor? Dr. Dorin, I suffer in private. I cry in private. When I was a kid, when I was coming of age, there was no one to celebrate that. No one ever gave a shit about me as a kid. I had the wrong kind of voice. I had friends with mellifluous voices; *mine* was always irritating. It hurt people's ears." And there had been silence, silence for a full minute.

"I have a young daughter with enormous appeal," Dr. Dorin had said. "I know I am her father, but I'm somewhat objective about it as I compare reports with my friends' kids. The counselors write from camp and say my daughter's kindness is engaging. They say things about her that portray her as a loving, caring young person. She's fat. She's quite fat. But she doesn't *have* to be fat. You see that's the good news.

You say you're always missing the sympathy on the first draft. In life that's *not* the only draft we get. Well, we've got to look for the good news. You've got to say what the assets of Jack Krenner are. What are the strengths of this man? Tell me about *that*, Jack. Tell me what's *good* about Jack Krenner."

Rolling down Loma Vista past his business manager's house, Jack remembered the horrible party with the model and one Russian wolfhound posing on a white Rolls-Royce, an entrance spectacle to a black and white theme bash. Guests dressed in black and white, the orchestra in black and white, the hors d'oeuvres in black and white. Everyone four thousand years old.

Now, morning doves on the night road and finally the escape lane at the bottom of the hill. A left turn. *There:* a woman loping along in blue jeans. She had huge thighs; not correct. Now down to the strip. Past Doheny, the billboards screaming. He wasn't certain what he would want. He would have to wait for the voice. The light winked on the telephone receiver, signaling that someone was on the phone at his home. Was Marjorie calling someone? Did she always wait until he left to call . . . perhaps a lover? He had had the complex transmitters installed at his house and in his car to listen to her, to listen to his wife and to hear the things she would say when she knew he wasn't home.

He lifted an ear receiver to his head, fitted it into place.

". . . I just finished the fourth chapter," he heard Marjorie's voice, "and I'm very hopeful. It's just a four-thousand-dollar advance, and mainly out of respect for Jack . . ."

Who was she talking to?

Finally, the other voice: "I envy you, Marjorie, I

really do. The rest of us say we're going to do something but we end up redoing the house or . . ."

Patricia. She was talking to her friend Patricia in New York.

Did Patricia call? Who would be paying for the bill?

"How's Louise and Joey?"

"Fine. How's Jack?"

"Fine."

Drive carefully. Don't attract attention. He hadn't taken enough cocaine to impair the driving, but just in case, he placed the vial with its cap and little spoon into a niche in the door. If the police did pull him over for a traffic violation, they'd never find it.

Finally, Marjorie hung up. He took the receiver from his ear, satisfied Marjorie wasn't talking about him behind his back.

9:00 P.M.

Another woman walking too swiftly. She has a goal. Now passing the street where Sal Mineo was murdered—there. Another woman, cheap, *wrinkled.* Oh, but what if a cop looked in his Adidas bag, looked below the towel and the shower slippers, and the cards, and miscellaneous accumulations of several years of health clubbing. What if he was pulled over for being in the wrong lane and the police wanted to look in the bag? But no, cops would be too busy on the Strip for minor traffic offenses. Perhaps he should circle. Perhaps there would be a stray young lady coming up one of the off streets, a *stoned* young lady. No, he'd go further on Sunset. There, another fat one. The Chateau Marmont. *Oh yes, Bobby D. stays there whenever he's in town. Oh, wonderful, would you leave this script for Mr. D.? If he reads it, that would be fine, but I wouldn't be hurt if he doesn't. I wouldn't be hurt.*

And there, TOTALLY NUDE. OUR GIRLS HAVE GOT IT AND THEY'RE GOING TO SHOW IT, OR YOUR MONEY BACK. Taste get your flowers get your Schwabs get your squabs at Schwabs . . .

A left on La Brea up to the Boulevard. The Boulevard delivers. Mummies on the streets, the retirement villages.

"Ladies, ladies. Where's my lady?"

He had brought the correct instruments to get what he wanted this time. And at that moment he began to hear the Voice inside of him, the strange low voice he had merged with at his mother's deathbed. The Voice, the stirring Voice which had been muted all his life—but now was growing, gaining strength to save him from his conscious pain.

And now the Boulevard, all the footprints and handprints in cement.

10:15 P.M.

He saw her, his girl. The Voice told him she would be his.

She climbed in: easy, young, a hitchhiker with a backpack, from Florida; a pretty face, liked to cook, was looking for a temporary job. She said she'd love to go out for a drink.

"There's a nice place in the Valley I know," Jack said.

"What's with all the electronic stuff?" she asked, looking over the set of dials and lights beneath the dashboard. "You're not a cop are you?"

"No. I'm a ham."

"A ham?"

"I'm into ham radio. I want to keep track of what's going on in other countries. I have a radio that can bring in a signal from Germany. Most of it's just CB equipment."

"Looks like a lot more than any CB I ever saw."

He liked the sound of her voice. He thought she looked and sounded like a young June Allyson. He was aware of the way she seemed to be deliberately spread-eagled and glassy-eyed on the comfortable tan leather of the front seat. As they passed street lights, he noticed her hair appeared strawberry blond.

"Some of my friends don't like older men, but I do." She talked on and on as he drove. He'd go to the freeway, *left* on the freeway.

"Yes, this is the famous freeway."

She was a nice girl, he told the Voice; she wanted to talk about her mother. Her mother didn't understand her. She became a blur as his own mother leapt into his mind. *"Help me, Jackie . . ."*

"The nurse . . . I'll call the nurse."

"Don't let them touch me, Jackie."

10:45 P.M.

Now get off at Laurel Canyon. Oh yes, his little passenger said, she'd love to see the hills. She'd heard so much about the hills. The more she talked, the lovelier and more misguided she seemed. His girl tonight was vain and selfish on the surface, but she could be redeemed. The Voice might listen to him.

"Do I turn you on?" she asked.

"Not much," he answered. "Why do you ask?"

"It just looks like you got something swollen in your pants, that's the only reason. If you really don't mind, and you like me, maybe we could do something and you could give me the money you would have spent on drinks."

Soon they were parked at the top of the canyon. A cold wind was blowing in from the Sierra Madre. The filth of the L.A. air had been kicked out to sea, and the city looked like a field of chandeliers.

"I could give you fifty dollars," he told her. "Forty and maybe another twenty—that would be sixty bucks."

"That would help me out a lot, mister."

"I want you to fellate me."

"What's that?"

"I want you to suck on me." He enjoyed just saying the words, and watched her reach over and unzip him.

"God, you are big, mister. Really big."

Watching her begin to take his organ in her mouth was close to human ecstasy as he could imagine. He knew the cocaine was mainly responsible, but there were other factors that lifted him beyond the considerable pleasures Marjorie gave to him. This strange woman sucking on him, moving her tongue clumsily around the corona, trying to take it all into her throat was more than he had hoped for. She seemed apologetic for not being able to let the end of his penis do more than smack and kiss the back of her throat. Did she know that there were enough women who were willing to engulf a man's organ until it would literally bend and push its way nearly to the vocal cords? This girl's newness, and the vast panorama of night beyond made him feel as though he were sitting on top of a space vehicle. He put his arms along the back of the seat and became an observer to the act. Her amateur fumblings, her attempts to please, were magnificent because they kept him just below the point of orgasm. He let her suck him for more than half-an-hour, and when she tried to lift her head to rest, to breathe, he gently guided her back onto him. He could feel semen collecting in his testicles. And with a short additional sniff of cocaine, he had a brief vision in which he became a reptile. He was a great astral throbbing body. Finally, to his surprise, the girl's efforts became totally passionate. She swallowed by accident in a way that allowed his cock head to thump still deeper into her throat. He knew she had just discovered the technique for totally devouring a large man, and the moment surpassed his greatest fantasies. The cocaine permitted his engorged cock head to thump no more than three, four times with heightened power, actually opening its mouth, the mouth of the cock head, kissing the deepest red of this strange girl's throat. The knot of white, hot fluid began to roll from his testicles and now his body became autonomous. He pressed her head so deeply onto him that he felt the first rush colliding against the back of her throat. She swallowed and the accidental swallowing became totally professional. He poured into her for more than a minute, completely unconscious of rational thoughts.

He finished by opening the car door and moving his left leg into a quick uncomfortable position while lifting the girl's head off him. His penis was hard, literally trembling and he knew there would be more. He took her out of the car. *Oh yes, the lights. We'll talk about the view and the lights, give her a chance to breathe.* That was good for a while, and then he had her against a tree. Occasionally a car would come along Mulholland, and its lights would flash for a moment across the turnout. They would hit the back of the tree. If a car stopped, and if its occupants strained they might notice a naked man pressing his girl against a tree. But he had wanted his clothes off, had stacked them neatly in a pile a good distance from where he had her, from where he was perpendicularly entering her. The clothes would remain clean and unsoiled. He needed the Adidas bag near him, and when she asked about it, he told her it was just in case they needed lubricant. And as he fornicated with her, only once did his depression float across his mind. *"Oh yes, I know we promised you the 3D, the comedy. 3D has never lost money, but I'm sure you know. Mr. Wilbert says the casting's all wrong. I'm sorry, Jack. Well, what does that mean? It means you're being replaced. This little yenta Gilda can't deliver from a studio in which the chief executive is a tight-assed faggot and the ex-football player president drinks from morning to night. And you tried so to educate them, Jack. This fine writer, I told them, Jack. Do you realize what you're doing to this fine writer? You asked the right questions, exposed the root of the problem. Yes, the expositions were a little long in your fine, fine screenplay, but the casting is wrong because his little girl, the secretary who is not a qualified script reader said the casting is wrong, and none of the executives read . . .*

Now, his mind was back with his lady against the tree. He knew she was thrilled. She had even stopped asking about money. His power lifted her up onto her toes, higher. Her eyes were closed. She didn't notice him reaching to the left of her to the bag he had set nearby, its mouth gaping wide. There was a change in rhythm that finally made her open her eyes. Then she became aware of something cold touching her lower stomach.

Her eyes opened wide now, staring at this man still inside her. A car passed on Mulholland and she saw his eyes clearly in the spill from its headlights. He moved a fraction out of her and somehow she knew he was inviting her to look downward. She twisted her head, her gaze falling and into the brief crevice between their bodies and saw the shining metal shape of a small surgical scissors pushing into her skin.

"Shhhh," he said. "I don't want to hurt you." And then the Voice: "I just want to talk to you."

She fought harder, thrashed. And he felt as though the top of his head were about to blow off with joy. *A dream, it's a dream.* The fluids mounted again in his testicles, and he pushed her higher onto the tree.

"Just be quiet. Or I'll cut *inside* you."

The girl stiffened into silence. He could even remove his hand from her mouth.

"Jeee-sus, Mister! Jeesus, Mister! Jesus, Mister."

She began to breathe, straining to look down to the curl of blood running from the white of her left thigh.

"I'll do anything else you want, Mister."

He pressed her harder against the tree, feeling as though his organ had crashed through her and into the living fibers of the tree.

"Why are you filthy?" the Voice asked her. "I need to know about your filth."

She began to explain her sinfulness, nearly incoherent. "Lake George, Lake George, Mister. Please, Mister. I was a waitress. Saratoga. Jimmy, the busboy, we went waterskiing between the breakfast and lunch setups. Please let me go let me go let me think. I was kept in a situation of inferiority. A little joke. A year at college. Don't cut. Please, don't cut me. I'll go wherever you go, any trip, drugs. You want drugs? Jeeesus, Mister! Another blow job, Mister, anything. Oh, Mommy, I'm sorry. It's hurting me. The scissors are hurting. Mister, this is bad. You're doing a bad thing. I know how you feel Mister . . ."

He was into her now with a feeling that made him remember a pimp he met once in Taos. A pimp who used to supply sailors to the brothels in Tijuana.

The sailors would pull out, and scrape a comb across the head of their organ and sprinkle it with cocaine and then go back in and feel they were fucking with a telephone pole, yessuh . . .

"Why are you melting?" the Voice asked her.

"What, Mister? What, sir?"

He wanted to tell her more of what the Voice was saying, but words became impossible. And in his final thrashing, she stayed hoisted, waited for his convulsing groin to stop. Then in a fairy tale she dreamed he would withdraw, get into his car and drive off, leaving her alive. Even the scissors dropped.

I don't want to do this but I'm doing it. I won't do it . . .

No. He stayed inside her.

After a long while he reached out to his bag for the final instrument.

Lichteiman got the call at four-thirty in the morning. A young Chicano and his girlfriend had decided to park off Mulholland and came across something nailed to a tree. At first they thought it was a scarecrow, but on closer inspection it proved to be the body of a young girl crucified, her entrails hanging from a gaping hole in her abdomen. The body had been ripped open; there was no other expression for it, Straub insisted. As Lichteiman acknowledged later at the morgue, the summation of the expert coroner was horrifyingly correct: the perpetrator first had sliced open the living woman with a surgically sharp instrument, and then plunged his fist into the body to pull forth what he wanted, with only the roughest idea of anatomy. Pieces of the cadaver were missing.

"What do you want to do?"

"Sleep," Lichteiman mumbled and hung up.

Sleep, the great problem solver. And dreams, the landscape of the mind where Lichteiman searched for madmen. Only the sleeping mind gave him equal footing with the psychopaths that stalked the land. Asleep, his subconscious was able to join with the insanity of the times. *I am sleeping, sinking. Sleep that knits up the ravell'd sleave of care . . .*

Sometimes even in a daydream he could manipulate the flow of information. The pain of needing to know an answer seemed to create a cerebral convolution, which spit out the correct information— along, of course, with considerable background static and false or useless information. Lichteiman, the adding machine. Lichteiman on the side of the Gods. Lichteiman beginning to process the latest human illness which poured across his desk and life. *A woman in Agoura had her dog buried in the casket with her when she died. The dog was buried alive. AP: German father and son went on trial Thursday for the ritual slaying of the female members of their family. Horad and his son, Eric, are members of a sect which believes the kingdom of David will arrive after women have been exterminated. "The Archangel Gabriel appeared to us and told us that we have to resurrect the kingdom. But that we cannot do it without first eliminating the female sex." The mutilated bodies of his wife and daughters were found December seventeenth in an apartment in Santa Cruz.*

Floating phone calls: "Oh yeah, he was just a jealous husband you know. He killed her by passing an electric current through her brain while she was asleep. Yeah, I sat in on the whole court case." Florence, Italy: A twenty-year-old Italian village girl and her illegitimate baby were drowned in a cooking pot of boiling water by

*her own family for refusing to reveal the child's father.
"Well, I tell you, I had to burn down the shed to get rid of
them, but it didn't do much good because only sixty
percent of them were destroyed. I saw at least thirty-four
demons, and they looked exactly like figures in picture
negatives. They infested my home." "Yes, after seeing the
program on television the two boys found a body in their
freezer. Their father had actually murdered a woman."
In Buffalo, police found a young woman's decapitated
body in the bathtub and her arms in the kitchen sink of
an East Side apartment on Sunday. Three suspects, including two high school students, were arrested ...*

Lichteiman in a dream. The end stages of our
world. "Did you question? Did you count all right,
Straub? What do you mean, he went parking with his
girlfriend and found her nailed to a tree? Yes, in Florida some bikers found a girl nailed to a tree. . . . All
together now, what is it that the Shadow knew? Well,
the Shadow knew that evil lurked in the hearts of
men. Of course, Jung and Freud sort of knew that too,
didn't they?

Even in dreaming, Lichteiman's mind was preparing a news release: Lichteiman, the name to be
included in each and every article for the newspapers.
Even the Beverly Hills gossip rags. DETECTIVE
CHARLES LICHTEIMAN IS IN CHARGE OF THE INVESTIGA-
TION ... ALL PERSONS WITH INFORMATION PLEASE CALL
278-1000, EXTENSION 217 ...

The ritual which had begun in a bathroom at a
nursery school would soon need a confessor. The
dancer on the killing ground would cry out for a witness, and Lichteiman would do everything possible to
be that witness. *Stop me—oh, God, please stop me before ...*

Before what? What would be the time, the numerology, of this illness? Christmas, Lichteiman considered. Christmas or the Jewish Holy Days or the anniversary of a Death. The woman-hater would need him soon.

CHAPTER NINE

Marjorie made Jack's favorite meal, roast turkey and a sweet potato pie topped with melted marshmallows. She arranged playdates for the kids, and even got Jack into the Jacuzzi for a relaxing soak. When she finished loading the dishwasher, she climbed into the Jacuzzi next to him, consumed with guilt. Perhaps it was just the hot water that weakened her, or maybe she sensed the time was proper for her to be weak. She could never sit in the vapors of the Jacuzzi without feeling she was back in ancient Greece or Rome. She had always been fascinated by that period of history, by the rather delicious aspects that no one ever spoke about anymore except myopic scholars desperate for a thesis topic. She herself had done a paper at Hofstra once on Greek housewives in 400 B.C. who three times a year would bolt from their husbands and houses to perform orgiastic rites on the mountains. She had tracked the maenads of Greek art and literature, showed how the frustrations of ancient women led them to these Dionysiac seizures where they would toss their heads back and expose their throats in forceful, shouting convulsions—to relieve the pain of not being men.

Jack seemed so relaxed in the Jacuzzi she felt she

could err. She wouldn't need the exact words. She'd just blurt it out, get it out.

"You've achieved so much, Jack, and I know on some level I probably have been jealous of it. I mean, I think that's normal in a marriage don't you? I guess somewhere watching you at your work there's some little voice in me that always has been saying, 'Oh, I want to do it too.'"

She waited. She'd said enough. If he was interested, if the time was right, he'd say something. She watched him release his grip on the sides and let his hands fall completely into the water. Now only his head lay on the surface.

"How do you think I feel about . . . the competition?" he asked gently without opening his eyes.

Marjorie tried to be honest. She would have to be honest. "I don't think you like it. Somewhere inside of me I know that. I think it bothers you. I think sometimes I've been too uptight, trying to claw out something for myself, or slipstream you too closely. I think it makes you crazy. I don't know how you would really ever take it if I ever became successful." And now the positive, because that was just as true. "You *are* very encouraging with my work."

"Do you think I feel you're a *threat?*"

"No. No, I don't think . . ."

She realized she had immersed her own body under the water to her neck. And now just their two heads protruded from the caldron. She had instinctively followed his body language.

"I mean," she continued. "I think we *do* compete in a lot of ways. If we were painting a wall, we would compete to see who rolled more area. In miniature golf, the games, I feel that we're competing. Whose line is straightest of them all? And even in games, facts—when I say I know something, I think we compete there." She was babbling again, but she'd let it just pour out. It might help them. It might help defuse the bomb, and bring them so close she could reach into his head and pull out the madness that had made him piss in her milk, her children's milk.

"I've been feeling terrible, Jack. I feel very guilty because I feel that I'm a big piece of what's wrong with you. I'm one of the pressures. I feel I've pushed you a lot of times." She laughed nervously. "I may think I'm doing all the right things, but I'm not."

She felt very close to tears. She moved closer to him, her hands reaching out past a powerful water jet. Finally, her fingers found his chest, and then his hand.

Clackkkkkity click!

Marjorie heard a faint tapping of branches against the window.

She rested her head on his shoulder and wondered how many of the noises had really been Jack. And what were *all* the noises? What else was he doing? What else had he done? The health club. All the nights he said he was going to the club. What time did he really come home? Who was this man, this man she was holding?

7:30 P.M.

The kids were back from their playdates and Jack agreed to play Space Armada with Danny. Marjorie could see Courtney felt very left out. She tried to get her into bed, but Court wanted to play too. Jack was being particularly abrupt with Courtney, Marjorie noticed. It just seemed Jack had more patience with Danny than he ever had with Courtney. She remembered when Danny was born, how excited Jack had been. He was in the delivery room, not because he had gone to the Lamaze classes with her; at the last minute he decided he *did* want to be in to see the baby come; the joyful amazement on Jack's face when the doctor lifted up the baby and pronounced: "It's a boy!" In her slight stupor from the spinal anesthetic, she watched her robed husband, eyes peering out between his mandatory face mask and hair cap. He moved with the team to watch the aspiration of his son's lungs. She saw Jack's pride as the cries of his son broke through the air. But she also remembered nearly two years later when the scene was repeated; she remembered her exaltation when the doctor lifted their second baby aloft and announced, "Your family's complete now; it's a girl!" Her eyes had followed the glistening young female with placenta being borne across the room to the aspiration crib. This time Jack did not close in for any tight inspection of the new arrival. Something about his posture, his eyes, that signaled Marjorie that he might be slightly disappointed. Then the long proof: it was always Danny he wanted to take with him. He was more patient when Danny interrupted work on a new novel. When Danny was learning sounds of words, Jack was more than willing to drill him on the phonetic cards. But Courtney would cry out that she would like to try to make the sounds and Jack would gently dismiss her, unconsciously put her down, eventually yell at her that Danny was older and it was his homework, not *hers*. For Courtney it was always supposed to be another time, a later time, a time that never seemed to come.

NOVEMBER 21
9:00 A.M.

The communication Lichteiman was waiting for finally came. Lichteiman had gone into headquarters

to check over the final lab reports on Terry Jane
Davidson, the rather pretty, naive daughter of a farm-
ing couple in the Napa Valley. He had heard a report
from someone on the force that Mrs. Davidson seemed
somehow pleased that her daughter had been found
disemboweled and nailed to a tree, as though it were
fit and proper punishment for leaving home. But Mr.
Davidson had cried.

Straub delivered the photographs personally to
Lichteiman's desk, the closeups of the gaping hole in
the girl's abdomen. Sad, low angle shots of this lady
Christ, then Straub's questions, his need to tap into
the Buddha of Lichteiman for consolation and solace.

"A rough way to make a living," Straub moaned.
"Do you ever regret you went into this business?"

Lichteiman smiled. "No regrets, and I don't owe
anybody a fucking thing." He snapped his fingers, and
with one look propelled Straub to reach out to the
coffee pot and pour him another cup while he looked
through the pictures. The package arrived that morning.

It had come through ordinary mail. It didn't look
like a bomb, and was brought to Lichteiman's desk at
11:10. There was something about the large black letters spelling out his name and the headquarters address that made him feel it was what he was waiting
for. He didn't mind the way Beverly Hills preferred to
downplay its freak crimes. As long as there was
enough of the story printed to let the perpetrators
follow their crimes. *Detective Lichteiman is handling
the case.* "Well, you see, there's no point getting everyone all worked up," the Commissioner always said.
"We're still reeling from Manson, and you know what
they do with the stuff back East. These girls might not
even be connected. This kind of trash hitchhikes and
gets picked up by truck drivers. Killers like this can

come right out of Watts and Burbank. We've got fucking Gucci, Hermes, Giorgios, Van Cleefs paying a fortune in rent and striped awnings. What we don't need is to put a bug up the ass of the ladies that some guy is going to follow them home and yank out their tubes . . ."

Lichteiman opened the package slowly. It was about the size of a cigar box, but not as sturdy. He sniffed the wrapping. No sign of any chemical or plastic explosive. The heavy brown wrapping paper fell away. With the wrappings off it became amorphous, translucent. The first impression was that of a sealed baggie with a dead eel. But now the plastic had ripped, and fluid leaked onto the desk. The stench made Lichteiman bolt up and back, let the rookies leap in on the evidence. The lab boys were called down, but not before Lichteiman had extracted a second sealed baggie containing a letter. He willed himself beyond the excitement and took the letter from its plastic covering as delicately as if he were handling uranium.

"From hell.

Dear Mr. Lichteiman

My kind sir, I send you half the ovary I took from her. The other piece I kept for a while, until it began to go bad. I fed it to one of the dogs. Women. I want to push my fist down their throats until they are dead. I saved some of her blood in a bottle, but it congealed and the smell makes me sick. It makes me sick in the same way I become sick when I think of what I was told to do with the next one. I want to slit her belly and reach in with both hands again, but I want to break the body apart. I want to break the woman in half. I want you to find the body severed. I need to feel the spinal column and crack it. I do this for the filth of women and when we meet (if I am dead) please know that I loved my wife and children.

Yours in bedlam,
Love"

CHAPTER TEN

DECEMBER 3

Marjorie thought Jack seemed much better after several weeks with Dr. Dorin. He didn't seem to want to talk about his sessions with the psychiatrist, and she didn't push it. She'd just ask how it was going, and Jack would say fine—that he was feeling much more in control and that he knew exactly what he'd have to do in order to solve his problems. Marjorie noticed he was even going out for drives and starting to talk optimistically about his projects. She hadn't forgotten about the cocaine, but somehow she was never able to really mention it again. A lot of writers and actors were using it. And he was spending several evenings each week out at the health club. Or so he said. . . . *No*, Marjorie thought, *I won't let myself turn suspicious.*

DECEMBER 5
9:00 P.M.

Marjorie decided to check her husband's desk. She felt guilty, as if pilfering ideas for her own writing, but told herself it was for Jack's benefit. A fire burned in the library hearth, and even though Marjorie knew Jack was at the club, she could feel his presence. The big desk's left drawers were locked, but

she opened drawers on the right and was surprised to
see a very small tape recorder. She didn't even know
he had such a thing. On top of the desk, in plain view,
was a recorder with standard cassettes, and something that looked like a suction cup with a jack. Next
she checked a large collection of standard cassettes.
They were labeled, organized. She was about to shut
the drawer when she was drawn to the label on one
stack. She pulled out one marked "Gilda" and put it
into the recorder. The small speaker began to cough
up static, then voices. Marjorie quickly realized she
was listening to a taped telephone conversation. First
her husband's voice and then his agent's.

GILDA: *Well, everybody's in trouble. None of that crap is
making money. At least the reviewers are finally tearing into Neil's little bulldog. Isn't that a riot?* An explosion of Gilda's laughter, more static. *Jack,
darling, I hope we're doing the right thing.*

JACK: *I think you're doing the right thing Gilda,
provided you document what they're doing to us. We
can sue.*

GILDA: *Somewhere little Harry is going to have a surprise. Are you pressured dear?*

JACK: *No.*

GILDA: *Good. I've been on the Pritikin diet. I've got a
new clarity of vision about the sons-of-bitches in that
studio. Jack, I tell you there are many people who love
you there. They all talk about your quality. What an
honor and what a prince you are among writers. I'm
really sorry about what they want to do to your script.
I don't know why they want to kill you. I told them to
cast Barbra and hump her, if that's what they want.
But just do the picture. They said no. Jack, they said
no!*

JACK: *Look, you can't shove me down their throats.*

GILDA: *They said your piece is too soft, that it needs*

more bite. And then crazy Tom says again, 'I want my boyfriend.' Harry's lover is going to take over your job. And then the head of the studio, the alcoholic says, 'Gilda, do you think we could have a meeting tomorrow?' So I'm supposed to meet with them, an alcoholic and the number two man, who is, I don't know how to describe it, a very ill, shameful man, a real prick who looks like he sits on chilled suppositories . . .

Marjorie thought she could hear Jack listening. His silence on the tape frightened her.

GILDA: *They've got that little girl over there who's killing everything. She's a secretary, and she's the only one that reads scripts. And she doesn't know what she's reading. She ends up writing these little paragraphs about how everything is shit. That's her whole job over there, to say 'no.' And they just move on whatever she says* . . .

JACK: *Gilda, I need a credit. I need a solid film credit for credibility* . . .

GILDA: *Yes, dear* . . .

JACK: *I'm losing another credit, Gilda* . . .

GILDA: *Jack, I told you I was shaking. I don't blame you for being sick* . . .

Marjorie listened. There was laughter now, a laughter beginning to dominate the tape. A series of loud guffaws and then, almost a hysteria. She recognized the laughter as Jack's.

GILDA: *Jack. I'm sorry I couldn't do more.*

Static. The laughter fading.

GILDA: *Jack, Jack, what's the matter? Jack, I can't hear you. Jack, are you crying? Jack, I'm sorry. I'm just so sorry.*

DECEMBER 9
3:00 P.M.

Lichteiman sat at his desk sipping a Tab, vaguely aware of the fact that one of the detectives was listening to music on a Sony Walkman. It was a faint drift—some high-voiced boy with a backup group singing about being lonely: "La de da. Doo be doo. You're sooo cru-elllll."

There had been nothing in weeks now. Not since the section of the girl's ovary had been received. The body tissues had matched up. Both had the same percentage of gin and glucose. The need to kill again had to be building, storing up like semen in the killer's body. There would have to be a release. Lichteiman wanted this Love character. He wanted Love to know his gift had been received, and the Times cooperated with a filler story: ALTER EGO CAUSE OF VIOLENCE was the headline. A little bit about a hillside strangler, a mention of Manson, the throat-slittings of a couple the year before in Bel Air. Most of the article was general, based on a report by Louis Goldman, a psychiatrist from San Diego. At the end of the rather calm article came the paragraph Lichteiman had ordered. A few prosaic sentences about one or two unsolved murders in the Los Angeles area. No specifics other than that Detective Lichteiman was in charge and had received a contact from the perpetrator. *"It is clear that the man needs help, and I'm hoping he'll contact me again," said Detective Lichteiman. . . .*

Lichteiman had decided much earlier in his career that a maniac is never caught by routine work. The routine has to be performed, but a true maniac like Love becomes known only when he wishes to be known. At the moment, Love was too bashful. His bloody gift was too hateful, too soiling. But it was a beginning. In time Love would want to reach out and embrace Lichteiman fully, Lichteiman believed. That's how it had always been.

Straub had drawn him out on the subject. "You're not going to catch him with clues, because nobody cares anymore!" Lichteiman had growled.

"Well that's *your* opinion."

"You bet your ass it's my opinion! If you ever really asked cops what they think of police work and the courts they'll tell you it's all chickenshit! It's chickenshit in New York! It's chickenshit in San Francisco! And it's chickenshit here! The courts, the lawyers, and the liberals have put goddamn wire nooses around our balls! You bet your ass I'm fucking mad! The maniacs are the last ones you've got to worry about. You can't stop anything anymore."

By noon a report had come in from Miami over UPI. It mentioned that an unidentified body of a young man had been found: his head, hands and legs had been cut off and were discovered Saturday night inside a house which police said resembled a torture chamber. The report said that the severed parts of the young man's body were discovered along with the torso. The boy had been stabbed several times in the groin. Detectives were checking the possibility that the remains were those of a young politician's son who reportedly disappeared last month. A student told detectives in Boca Raton last week that he and another boy had been picked up at a bar and taken to a home in the southwest Miami area. He reportedly made a statement that they were both sexually abused and his friend murdered. There was apparently no attempt to locate the house at that time.

"Not our man," Lichteiman said.

"Why not?" Straub asked.

"Our man is into something else."

DECEMBER 10
2:30 P.M.

Another package arrived for Lichteiman. This one had the weight and size of a book. There was the possibility that it could have been rigged with a bomb. It was opened, declared safe, and forwarded to Lichteiman's desk. Lichteiman pushed apart the already opened, brown-paper wrapping and found himself looking at a VHS Hitachi T-120 video cassette. He poured himself his fifth cup of coffee for the morning, grabbed a couple of Seasoned Rye Krisps from a fat rookie's desk and took the cassette up to the media room on the second floor. The air inside the room was stale with smoke and carbon dioxide left over from a class in weaponry. On a blackboard were chalk cross-section drawings of dum-dum bullets. He put the cassette into the video recorder and sprawled onto a couch to watch the show.

At first the screen only flashed with the white-and-black speckled ghost of blank tape. He waited, and when no image appeared, he pressed the rapid forward switch about eight feet into the tape. A picture faded in, though he couldn't figure out what it was at first. The camera was pointed at something—shadows, holes of light. The objects moved, then came into focus. Lichteiman made out a section of rug, a piece of white in the right corner of the picture. Some sort of greenery hovered in the background, as though beyond a window. The camera was aimed at the floor. A man's bare foot slid into the frame from the left, then a portion of both legs, halfway up the calves. Sound now—a distant noise of birds and one hiss of breathing, normal inhalation and exhalation. And then the voice—

"I need to talk to you . . ." the voice began. "I need to . . ."

Lichteiman's brain computer began to catalogue, toss out, zero in, correct, move, view, search, hook into the voice, the age. Madmen had sent him audio cassettes before, but this was Lichteiman's first video. He looked at the hair on the legs, checked for calluses on the feet, the toenails, the background, the trees. *Where is it? Who is it?*

"I tried visualizing my pain," the voice went on slowly. It was strained, barely a whisper now. "There's a large fish tank in my head. I tried to let the black fluid run out. I'm ill, Mr. Lichteiman. My doctor has told me . . . so much mental juggling to do, so much . . . and I'd thought I'd found a temporary salve. I've thought about going to a cemetery . . . I need to get at the cause in me. I know . . . feelings, feelings not thoughts. Sometimes my feelings make me think I'm having a heart attack or cancer. The feelings make it very real for me. . . . My cauldron, as the doctor calls it. I have a strong set of feelings . . . I have pain in my head, Mr. Lichteiman . . . the left side of my face is growing numb, and it is very frightening. It builds. It's building again, Mr. Lichteiman. I feel as though I have to go somewhere and do something again. It's not me. I've pushed the voice down for a while. There are pieces of me that are missing. It's not up to me to . . . live . . . them . . . don't the cunts have feelings? If they don't like me, it's going to be a two-way street. The burden isn't on me anymore . . ."

The voice stopped. The picture continued. The feet. The dark hair on the legs. White marble. Probably his home. Wine carpet, large room, tan tile strip near large picture window. Lichteiman's imagination pushed, stretched, shot imaginary parallel lines out from the images on the screen to extrapolate the environment. Beyond the tile was lawn, lawn with shadows, shadows of trees. Out-of-focus tree forms: eucalyptus trees, wide, large, peeling, vines filling an expanse between lawn *and . . . something*. Large backyard. Good materials. Money. The man's legs vibrating, shaking slightly. The feet moving slowly apart. Other sounds. Change in breathing.

Love's voice: "My daughter . . ." The voice weaker, lower, still capped, straining for matter-of-fact tone. "The girl is getting bigger, growing. My wife thinks I don't have feelings for her, but she doesn't know about my feelings for her. I cannot show my feelings all the time. I am not failing her. I keep the hallway lit and a dog sits near her room. I've trained him to sit in case someone comes to try and hurt them. The dog could rip out the throat of anyone who wants to harm them. There is another dog, and a few rabbits. They are watching me. They don't like me. When my daughter cries I know my wife is wondering why I don't do something to stop it? Why am I making her sad and causing her to cry? But my wife has feelings that go against me now. I think they're feelings from nature, that the children come first. My children are lovely. My girl leans forward and kisses me. My girl loves me when my wife isn't there. And she feels my feeling. When she looks at me, I can tell she forgives me. I don't have much more to say. I don't know much more. I'm sorry I have to speak to you, Mr. Lichteiman, but I know I'm going to have to do what I said I would . . ."

Christmas.
Lichteiman could smell Christmas. It brought to

mind the pain in Love's voice, the desperation. The holidays . . . the deadly catalyst of holidays. Christmas was coming and he had no suspects. In San Diego, in 1976, Lichteiman had helped narrow down a list of suspects because one had a wife called Natalie. There had been mutilations, attacks building through November and into December. There had been notes from the woman-hater detailing his hate, that he would kill her on her birthday. It was Lichteiman who picked out the husband of Natalie . . . *Natalie*, from the Latin *natalis*: "natal, or birth day." *Natalie*, the favorite name for girl children born on or near the greatest of Christian holy days . . .

Will you kill them all, Love? Lichteiman wondered.

CHAPTER ELEVEN

DECEMBER 14
10:00 A.M.

Standing in front of one of the huge picture windows of the master bedroom, Marjorie watched Jack put the finishing touches on the kids' tree house. She was happy to see him hammering away, lugging the boards up with Tomás's assistance. She knew the physical activity would relieve his inner tensions. Tomás did most of the dangerous work, climbing high, holding the boards of the roof in place while Jack hammered. This was the first day the kids had been allowed to climb up the rope ladder and walk about, taking possession of their new residence.

11:00 A.M.

"How do you like it?" Jack asked, as he moved inside the tree house to begin flattening the hundred or so roof nails which had broken through.

"Daddy, what's the spookiest thing that ever happened to you?" Courtney asked. She sat in a corner with her first furnishing for the tree house, an elaborate plastic tea set.

"I don't know," Jack said.

"What's the spookiest thing that ever happened to *you*?" Danny asked Courtney.

"Oh, there was this movie one day when I came home from school—Daddy was inside and I came in and put on the television—and this girl was there and she killed people with a knife, anyway it looked like a knife. And at the end she is captured by the police. See they had gone to this place and gotten food and this man saw one of his friends and they finally stuck her. And then they were in a church and this guy saw that it was his girlfriend that did the killing and then he went back outside and told some other guys, 'Hey, I know that girl. She's a killer.' And then the police came in, but she cut a priest's throat before they took her to jail."

"I don't want you watching that stuff, Courtney," Jack said, still hammering away at a corner where the nails had gone totally astray.

"They got worse stuff in picture books," Danny said, laughing.

"What's the spookiest thing you ever read in a fairy story?" Courtney asked Danny.

"I don't know."

"Well, it's Sleeping Beauty," Courtney said loud and clear. "Do you know about Sleeping Beauty, Daddy?"

Jack had to smile, "Yes, I've heard of her."

"Well you see there was this girl," Courtney began as she tried another arrangement of teacups and saucers. "She was a beautiful girl and her name was Sleeping Beauty. She had a mother and father once upon a time. And her mother's name was Clara and Daddy's name was Jake."

"That's very nice," Jack admitted. "I never knew what her parents' names were before."

"She's lying," Danny pointed out.

"I'm not lying, stupo. Clara and Jake took good care of Sleeping Beauty until one day, when she lived in the castle something happened. She took a walk and met her fairy godmother. Her fairy godmother told her, 'You must get cleaned up. Put on a beautiful dress. A new beautiful dress.' Then Sleeping Beauty got a new beautiful dress and she started saying, 'Thank you very much.'"

"Get to the good part," Danny urged.

"Well she's walking along and she sees this beautiful house. She thought it was her grandmother's house. So, she knocked on the door to see if she could take a rest. 'Who's there?' came this voice. 'It's Sleeping Beauty,' Sleeping Beauty said. When she opened the door there was a coyote! A coyote with a spinning wheel."

"My teacher at school is a *wolfman*."

"And that's the end of Sleeping Beauty," Courtney said.

From below, near the base of the eucalyptus trees, Samson started to bark wildly.

"Oh, shut up," Danny yelled down, pulling up a long rope with his knapsack tied to the end. He sat in the corner of the tree house now, playing Pac Man without a sound. "Do you think Sam ever cries?" Danny asked his father.

"What do you think?" Jack asked.

"Oh, I think dogs do," Courtney interrupted.

"I think dogs cry when their wives get killed."

"Or when their children get killed," Danny said.

Jack laughed. "Do you think Samson would ever like to go out to a restaurant?" he kidded.

"Ohhhhhh," Courtney giggled. "They'd like to go out to an animal restaurant, but not a person restaurant. They need a sign that says only dogs allowed."

"Do you think Samson loves Sandy?" Danny asked.

"Oh, I think so, because they got married," Courtney answered. "I think they'd like to go to a dinner dance," Courtney giggled uncontrollably. And Danny joined in. They laughed so hard the tree house shook.

"What would you do if a wolfman tried to come up to your tree house?" Jack asked.

Danny looked up at him. Courtney became very pensive and thoughtful.

"I'd beat the hell out of him," Danny said.

Marjorie was amazed that Carole Bender stayed so long with Rajweesk Bhagree Swahn. Whenever she and Marjorie were out shopping or going for a lunch, she found Carole quoting her newest guru. "In a Tantra coitus you can remain for hours with your entire vaginal area pulsating. He has told me that the goal is to be so completely instinctual, so mindless, that we as women can merge with our ultimate destiny . . . that we as women can vaporize and become great passageways for the supreme, and during this coitus the man actually disappears in our arms and becomes a similar door for the supreme. That's how he defines sexuality. That's what is considered basic Tantra sexuality. It's a return to our great innocence. The absolute oneness when we were pure as children and could see love and sex, male and female for what they have always been. And I've got a great past-life reader for you, Marjorie. You must go to him. You'll find out what it's all about."

Marjorie had often been shocked by the bizarreness of the Beverly Hills idea of a "search for Truth." The man who had done the geology report on their house had confessed to her that sugar was the ultimate culprit in the world. To show how correct the psychic nutritionists were, he said, all one had to do was lie on the floor and put a Hershey bar on his chest. A Hershey bar on the chest would cause complete debilitation, complete powerlessness and immobility. Chocolate is the demon of our times, he had told her.

DECEMBER 16

Carole took Marjorie to lunch at Le Bistro and had one of her psychics join them. Marjorie didn't like the idea at all, but was pleasantly surprised when the psychic turned out to be a very pretty, sweet young woman called Miss Gow. And Marjorie didn't mind most of the mumbo-jumbo conversation between Carole and the psychic. With her custom sunglasses and two-carat solitaire, Miss Gow seemed firmly rooted in reality. The mumbo jumbo had something to do with Tarot cards and lighting candles, but it all seemed to be good-natured and rather amusing. Marjorie didn't even mind lingering with Miss Gow over coffee while Carole went up the street to hit a sale. Marjorie even asked her if she could tell her anything about what the hell was wrong with all the men in the world.

"Perhaps," Miss Gow smiled. "I think most of the male spirits on earth now are very insecure with how they exist in relationship to the female. They are appalled, these male spirits. They believe that most of what is female wants to be male. And most of what is male wants to be female. Men are confused. They are hurt, resentful, and insecure. They are, in the deepest spiritual sense, lost. The entire women's movement is not something new, but part of the cycle which has happened before. In order to understand this movement it has to be seen in political terms, in terms of evolution, and in terms of overpopulation. It is also best perceived in relationship to designs from the spiritual world which few humans on earth can consciously know."

"What do you think makes a husband want to hurt his family?"

"Hurt? Or do you mean *kill*?"

"Why do you say kill?"

"I feel a dark aura about you. It is caused by this matter you speak of now."

"Would you answer my question? Why would a husband want to hurt his family?"

"Well, it could be a lot of things. The destructive aspect of all of our existences contains many complex impulses toward growth. When this impulse becomes violently destructive, we must perceive it as a spirit which is let loose. A spirit escaped from the light. What you must see is that killing is a creative act. Murder and mayhem are acts of creation gone berserk. Creation gone haywire. We know in the spiritual world there have been a great many men who have murdered their entire families. And we see it as an indication that a certain level of pain has been reached by these husbands and fathers. The idea that we only hurt the ones we love can often become expressed as the fact that we *murder* those that we love. All you have to do is look into your own life and you will see how often you have hurt those you love yourself. Sometimes you find yourself deeply involved with a person, overwhelmed with feelings, immense feelings that cannot be correctly interpreted by the conscious mind. Often the most dangerous feeling is that of inadequacy, for failure in the eyes of love can be a very great hurt. Often, when a man stands and compares himself to the universe, there is a deep mayhem in his spiritual soul. Love is the great source of confusion. Today many men feel their manhood is stifled. They have to engage in a ferocious fight in order to keep the mere sexual dimension of manhood alive. Often these men become satyrs, conducting an extraordinary sex life in order to keep in touch with that manhood."

"What will *my* husband do about it?" Marjorie asked directly.

"Your husband would like to do something great," Miss Gow said quietly. "He does not believe in hope any more. He sees hope as an illusion, Marjorie. He has been a dreamer all his life, and he believes his only hope is action. He has not found dreaming very effective. I see your husband's card, Marjorie. Would you like to hear what it is?"

"Yes."

"Your husband's card is the swords ace. I see a hand issuing from a cloud, grasping a sword, the point of which is encircled by a crown. Your husband's card is a card of triumph. The excessive degree in everything, conquest and triumph by force. Your husband's card is a card of great force in love as well as in hatred, and your husband's card lies in greatest proximity to pentacles nine. This card provides the answer for you, Marjorie. It is a woman with a bird upon her wrist, standing amidst a great abundance of grapevines in the garden of a manorial house. It is a wide domain suggesting plenty of all things." Miss Gow took a deep, fast breath. Marjorie felt a tension filling the air and somewhere in the restaurant she heard dishes falling, breaking.

"Why did you stop?" Marjorie wanted to know.

"I stopped because of a vision, a very chilling and terrible vision."

"What is it?"

"Are you sure you want to know, Marjorie?"

"Yes," Marjorie said with annoyance.

"I see what your husband wants from you."

"What?"

"Your womb. Your husband wants your *womb*."

DECEMBER 20
MIDNIGHT

Something . . .

Sounds. Marjorie lifted her head up from the pillow at the frightening roar from the intercom.

The nightmarish resonance of the monster's steps heading for the bedroom. Faster. A crying boy. Something horrible coming, like angry dead stampeding from a mausoleum. Danny was screaming. This was more than a nightmare, some sort of hysterical begging.

Jack. Jack's voice. Jack angry. Courtney crying.

"Jesus! God! What's going on? *What's wrong?!*"

Marjorie's mind struggled toward full consciousness. A moment later she was out of bed, racing across the white rug of the bedroom. Danny flew into her, spinning, slipping and falling onto the floor. He pulled his mother to her knees, screamed for her to come back up the hall.

"Hurry, Mommy! Hurry! *Daddy's doing something*. He's doing something!"

Where is Sam!

Courtney's voice bleating from the speaker: "No, Daddy! No! Please don't Daddy. No!"

Sam! Sandy! Where is Sam?!

Marjorie catapulted herself down the remainder of the hall. Adrenaline nearly split her heart. Tearing through, under the great chandelier of the center hall—then the last few steps of the west-wing hallway to the doorway of Courtney's room. Her arm crashed against the portal molding, stopping her, letting her ricochet into the bedroom.

She gasped, then froze in deadening shock as the screamings and the boomings quieted into a shiver and she beheld the sight on the doll-house bed.

Courtney lay on her back, her head held upon the arm of her naked father. They were both staring up at her, Courtney weeping, frightened, unable to move as Jack wedged against her. He had her legs apart like those of a small doll, being held open, spread apart. She reached her small hand out into the air.

"Mommy! Mommy!"

Courtney dazzled with fear, shaking while Jack clutched her tiny bone-white shoulders. He kept his head against hers and spoke.

"I want to be inside her. I want to be inside her, her . . . her!" Jack whispered.

Tears ran down his face. He looked puzzled, pathetic. "Help me. Oh, help me. I want to be *inside* her . . ."

Marjorie moved swiftly. Her arms flew around Courtney. She lifted her up and pulled her free, nearly hitting her own head on the canopy bar. She paused, needed to rearrange her grip on the child. Now the barking dogs.

"I want me in her, my cock right in her, in her pussy . . ."

He arched his nude body upward, forward, offering his manhood—a pleading gift of his genitals. He reached forward, grabbing his organ, beginning to masturbate violently.

"Let me come on her, please let me come on her . . ."

Marjorie hid Courtney's face in her bosom, and fled the room with her. She got Danny. There would be no clothes. No time to dress. Down the stairs, the turning spiral of black wrought iron, through the den, into the kitchen, the car keys. *Where are the car keys?*

Jack's voice, his pleadings on the intercom: "Help me. Don't leave me, Marjorie. I want to be in her. I want in her . . ."

Marjorie found her keys in the top drawer of the kitchen desk. She stumbled, rushed across the linoleum up the back stairs. The half set of stairs. The door to the garage. She opened it. Pressed the Genie. The garage door opened, the light clicking on automatically.

The Volvo. Outside. The dogs tied up somewhere, *barking,* angry.

Fast.

She yanked open the door of the driver's side, shoved Danny across to the far seat. She climbed in behind the wheel, shut the door. Courtney was still draped across her like a banner as she pushed the key into the ignition. The engine started, then stalled. She started it again.

Sam and Sandy barking . . .

Now she was backing out onto the street, putting on the brights. As she moved forward in a circle, the glare of the headlights hit the windows of the guest room and flowed along the white stucco. There in the next window, with the wooden shutters pulled back, framed by a bookcase of dolls, stood her husband. He was weeping, a begging mime as he pressed himself against the glass. His penis was enormous, flattened against the hard transparent window, and he was crying uncontrollably as his semen flowed upward, painting the glass.

CHAPTER TWELVE

MIDNIGHT

Lichteiman couldn't sleep, never could in a full moon. He didn't keep track of the lunar phases but, even if he was in London at a hotel, or fishing in Canada—it didn't matter where—he'd be in his room, trying to sleep, then feel as though his body was flooded with caffeine. He'd toss for three, four hours, then it would dawn on him. He'd get out of bed in the dark, pull down his nightshirt, go to the window. Opening the curtains, he'd look up into the sky and there it would be—the full moon. If it was overcast, he'd check. Always, in times of that nocturnal quivering, it would be the full moon. And it was nothing mystical or special, not worth writing about to all those scientists who were debating lunar effects. It was just a fact of life, and on those nights the only thing he could really do was get drunk. And his drunk was always the same: two bottles of Korbel champagne.

Lichteiman remembered the full moon shortly after midnight, and had started drinking. He went outside to sit on the edge of the stone wall of his canyon home. One benefit of his weighing so much, he'd found, was that no matter what he ate or drank now, he didn't put on any more weight. He always kept a twenty-seven-dollar Capachino mousse in the freezer, would chip off a huge piece topped with a leaf of white chocolate. The second bottle of Korbel was already chilling in a silver-plated champagne bucket he'd picked up at a garage sale for seven dollars. And tonight there was a double reason to get a good load on. Oh, there was the moon and the peaks of the Santa Monica mountains protruding above a middle tongue of fog, but below and beyond that, half of the city was ablaze with lights. Far off he could see planes landing at the airport and the condominiums glowing in Marina del Rey. On the south horizon was Palos Verdes, said to be gradually slipping into the sea, and beyond that Catalina. *Catalina with its sharks and Natalie Wood* . . . Yes, tonight might be the double drunk: the time of the full moon and the time of his madman.

There was enough of Love in his computer, in the convolutions of his mind. And soon, after a few more sips of champagne, the molecules of ethyl alcohol would be journeying wildly enough in his brain to let him drift into visions not terribly distant from those of the insane. Oh yes, crazy. Not of sound mind. Mentally deranged. Of actions idiotic, irrational, mad: *We have eaten of the insane Root that takes the reason prisoner.* Hell, Lichteiman knew he resolved most of his crimes with a good jag on. And when he was drunk, he had the habit of talking to himself. Sometimes he'd tell himself jokes and laugh. *Hey, listen, did you hear the one about this guy who makes a bet at the racetrack and as his horse runs he keeps screaming, "Please God, let him win!" "Please God, let him win!"—but in the home stretch the horse is ahead by twenty-seven lengths and he yells up to heaven, "Okay God, I'll take it from here." Har Har Har. Well, listen, Straub—you good-looking, sandy-blond schnook—"You think you're so hot Straub? University of Ohio School? What are you doing tonight, Straub, with your mouse-wife Jeanette and your sleeping sons? You're asking me why? You think it's about time I knew something about the motivation? You think it's about time I should be coming up with something that's going to get our man?"*

Lichteiman filled his goblet and looked out, down to the middle layer of fog which still cloaked only the canyon slopes.

I think you're in there, Love. I think you and your eucalyptus grove are down there. And what was that good old Friar Cherubino of Siena always used to say? What was that he said in his rules of marriage? . . . "Scold her sharply, bully and terrify her . . . readily beat her so that the beating will rebound to marriage and her good." Who are you really ripping, my Love? Oh yes, we know your victims. We know the kind of person you select. The one you slice and dip into. The weak and dependent, women with few resources for flight or retaliation. My, how you enjoy them. But behind those bloody go-betweens, my Love, who is the real target? Wherever you are down there, with your eucalyptus and your naked feet, when you mutilate, who is the imaginary figure receiving the scalpel? Whose interior are you really folding? Beating? Somebody who seems to be critical of you? Someone who's making it too hot in the kitchen? Who is your fantasy target, my Love? Perhaps you have Hate on your mind. But to me you want to be known as Love. Well, I understand, m'boy. You are going backwards . . . and you will be my child . . . my son . . . and I will be your father . . . I will be your someone strong, someone to believe in, to tell you the rules and to punish you. I will be your authority, m'boy . . .

Right now, you're building to something. And I won't really be able to stop you, will I? You want me to understand that you loved your wife and babies, but will they be alive to tell me it was true?

And now I'm so drunk I see you clearer than ever. I'm still waiting. I'm waiting . . .

12:10 A.M.

"What's the matter with Daddy?"

"Is Daddy crazy?"

"Why did Daddy say the F-word?"

The children were recovering. "Everything is going to be all right," she kept saying to them. "Everything is going to be all right." She pushed a cassette of children's songs into the Volvo's tape deck, turned on the heater.

At the top of Valley she veered right down Coldwater and into the marine fog which had just begun to crawl up the canyon. "Put your seatbelts on! Danny, put your seatbelt on!" She reached across her divinities, helped with the buckles.

"I'll do it, Mommy. I'll do it," Danny insisted.

She hunched over the wheel, speeding, watching every curve. *Pump the brakes, don't hold them steady, so they won't begin to bleed or sweat and disappear.* Her body was hot now with the blast of heat from the gaping vents and her breathing came in short, quick gasps. The exhilaration of escape suddenly gave way to terror again. What if Jack had somehow gotten out of the house and into the Seville? What if he were in the Seville coming from behind? With his eight cylinders against her meager four, he would catch her at any moment.

She checked the rearview mirror again and again, dreading to catch the reflection of two bright burning eyes. She thought of the owls that flew down and grabbed cats, huge birds that plunged their talons into soft furry bellies and flew high, two hundred, three hundred feet, before releasing their prey to fall to the pavement in a silent death. And then the owl would descend . . .

"C is for cookie, it's good enough for me . . ."
"Mommy, is Daddy going to be all right?"
"Mommy, can you rewind the tape?"
". . . tell us how to get to Sesame Street . . ."
Check the side mirrors. Headlights! Were those headlights behind her? No.

She sounded the horn as she rolled onto Beverly Drive, blasting the horn and screaming "Police! Police! Help!" But there were no police. There were no cars. There was no one walking on the street. And what made it even worse, she didn't even know if she really wanted the police.

"Why do you want the police, Mom?"

"I don't know, Danny." She needed something more than police. Something *other* than police.

Now she was frightening them. She was scaring the hell out of her own kids. She'd have to get herself under control. She groped around with her right hand without taking her eyes from the road. She pressed the glove compartment button. The little door sprung down revealing a bag of Tootsie Rolls. She had remembered the Tootsie Rolls. And there was always gum. She would calm down for them, if nothing else. Yet her mind was out of control. He would never get near the children again. She had the children safe. She would stay out; never go back. Her brain advising her: *My husband is out of his mind. I can never rest. I cannot be near him. I don't care if it's a cancer in his head. My husband with the beautiful dark hair, and the deep loving eyes, loving eyes, loving and pitiful. His help-me eyes.*

She felt nauseated. She thought about stopping the car, throwing up. She thought about running up to one of the homes. Even driving up to the Beverly Hills Hotel. She'd drive up the long archway, see the doorman. There were so many cars parked, lights glowing, the hotel ablaze. She would pull up and everyone would see the mother and children in night clothes. The mother and children without their husband father. "Help us! Help us!" she could cry to them, but she knew what they would feel. They would feel an appalling embarrassment.

She drove past Sunset into the flats, continuing down Beverly. *I'll take them to a friend's house. What friend? I'll leave my children at a friend's house. I need someplace. I need somebody. Someone who won't suspect. They'll put him into an institution. He needs to be locked up. He will be locked up. He'll get help . . .*

The full moon threw shadows from the palm trees across the road pavement. It created a stroboscopic effect as she rode over them. *I am in an amusement park. This is a fun house, an excruciating, painful fun house. I'll call his psychiatrist. He'll tell me what to do. The children are looking at me. Turn the volume up. Sing. Sing with them.*

"Sing. Sing a song . . . Sing out loud . . ."

My children out. He's not following me. He had no gun, no knife. It had to be a tumor. They can cut open his skull and take it out. My husband without a piece of his brain. Without the bad thing.

There were people now, laughing, a valet parking cars in front of La Scala. A small crowd near Haagen-Däzs. Valet parking at the Bistro Garden. Now she was crying, tears slipping down her face, but the children were singing. Worried, but singing. She didn't audibly sob. *I need help. I need help. I can't handle all of this. I'm not in charge of it.* The salad bar at R.J.'s. At this corner, oh yes, that's where Madeline K. passed her by one day. And on that corner she'd actually seen Fred A. and one of the Hardy Boys in line at the market. The boutiques. *Help me. Now help me. I'm the one that needs the help, not you. Not you. Not another sale.*

The computer teller at First LA Bank. Oh yes, I'll stick my card in, punch in my identification. And now, the world renowned Paris Institut, Florence Bouvier offers you bathotherapy, the new slimming program by jet streamed tubs . . . Oh yes, have you had their chicken salad? My husband wrapped in cellophane with Liza Minnelli and Joel Grey opening at the Greek. And there the shop where Neil Simon and Marsha looked in. And what do I do, my God! What do I do? Jesus Christ! What do I do? If she went to her neighborhood he'd find them. He'd go to Carole's first. A place for the children. Someone.

Joan Barron from the Roxbury Nursery School!

Joan, someone Jack would never think of. She turned the wheel of the Volvo. Benedict Canyon. She'd go up Benedict Canyon. But just past Sunset she noticed headlights in her rearview mirror. She did a left on Lexington, a right on Roxbury, but the car was still following them.

12:18 A.M.

Jack lay on the floor in the middle of the toys. Finally, he got up, managed to hold his body upright, then moved down the hall past the foyer and into the master bath. The amount of cocaine he had stored in a plastic bag was now considerable and valuable. He had moved it into a hiding place in the pocket in his ultrasuede sports jacket, along with a bottle of pharmacy-pure Quaaludes he had bought for the "final" event. He had already ground the Quaaludes in the coffee grinder; over three hundred tablets were now white dust. He knew it was time to mix the two whitenesses, so he poured the Quaalude powder into the bag of cocaine. He set the bag on the sink and began to stir, mixing the dazzling, elegant crystals.

His pain became too great. He tasted the whiteness before moving his body onto the bed. For a while
he lay on his back, head on a soft pillow. He opened
his mouth, but the scream caught in his throat. He felt
if he allowed the scream to emerge, it would go on
and on through infinity and perhaps be heard on the
moon. Instead, his body began to shake and the tears
came, heaves, gulps, deep cello moans.

And then he lay silent, afraid he actually *had*
screamed. That someone might have heard. Miss
Maggie could be skinny-dipping just beyond the fence
and wall of oleanders. There was a new secret sound.
A breathing. *Someone else is in the room breathing*, he
thought at first. *Or is something on the roof? No, it's
the heater.* The heater was on, pouring hot air down on
him from two vents.

He had never felt such a feeling of shame. *I love
you, Marjorie. I love you, my wife and children.* He
thought vaguely that he should leave the house because there was some danger. A part of his mind reminded him that he'd gone too far. But then, inside of
his brain, a whore came to him. He was awake, yet
dreaming. He was innocent in his own house, and the
whore was molesting things. *She isn't listening to my
orders . . .*

12:20 A.M.

The car followed her onto Benedict Canyon. She
didn't want the children to sense her fright as the
Volvo's engine strained up the canyon climb. The car
behind was gaining on her. *Move it! Move, car!*

The car behind was still gaining, faster.

She thought about pulling into a mansion driveway, but she knew that ended at a locked gate. She
thought about turning up Hillside. *Too many dead*

ends. She'd get trapped. She didn't know the area well enough. And then there was Ciello—no good, too steep.

The lights behind now closed in on her, huge mesmerizing white globes, as though she were at the end of a runway with a jet about to run over her. She was on the verge of crying out when the car passed her. A couple of Mexicans took a quick look at her. She thought she saw just a brief curl of disappointment on their faces during the split second they were beside her. Now she slowed, watching their tail lights pull off the road ahead of her. She saw them make a U-turn and head back down the canyon. She had forgotten the way the rich were robbed in that area. The Mexicans hadn't seen what kind of car she was in. They probably thought it was a Rolls or Mercedes at a distance. And they were probably desperate, since she was the only victim available at that time of night. They had hoped to follow her home if she had looked like she was worth any money. They would have let her press the remote control, and when the garage door opened they would have followed her in or gotten her against the house. . . . She turned around and headed back down Benedict Canyon.

Joan Barron would be perfect.

Joan in Bel Air with her husband Hal and their children Jake and Jenny. They were ex-New Yorkers. Hal was always off skiing and trying to hustle up investment dollars in the Napa Valley or someplace. Joan, who hated California and felt put-upon, somehow was very competent even though in a frustrating position similar to Marjorie's—of being a woman with little training for a career. She also filled the most necessary requirement at 12:54 in the morning: Joan was the kind of woman Marjorie knew could handle an emergency.

She took her shortcut across Camden, where one of the mansions was ablaze, a film crew working away. She made a right on Sunset. Courtney had fallen asleep with her head on Marjorie's lap. Danny made himself comfortable on the floor right under the heater. He loved any sort of cover. His tent. His tree house.

"Mommy? What's wrong with Daddy?"

For a moment Marjorie couldn't answer. It was like he had asked *why do we eat lamb chops?* or *how do X-rays get through your mouth and make pictures of your teeth?*

"He has a sickness, Danny," Marjorie said gently, reaching down to give his head a little scratch. "Sometimes our brains get sick and we need a little medicine, and then everything works out okay. Your father really loves you and Courtney very much, but it's just this *sickness.*"

"Are you going to help him, Mommy?"

Her mind stopped at that question. She had to force her human thoughts up through layers of primordial black leeches.

"Yes, I'm going to help him," she found herself saying.

Danny too was asleep by the time they passed the Bel Air gates. They stayed on Sunset a bit further, passing the UCLA campus. She had to watch for Club Drive. She turned too early and found herself on the maze of roads which crossed and crossed again into the Bel Air hills. Luckily, she found the one landmark she recognized every time she went to Joan Barron's house: a great brick English manor house that Dean Martin had owned. Then Tom Jones had bought it, and shortly after John Lennon had been murdered they had built the largest brick wall around the home that she'd ever seen. It now looked like a medieval fortress. She found Stratadella Road and finally arrived at Joan's house.

She pulled into the driveway and her headlights hit the beds of roses and lillies. A few lights were on, and she saw a deer bolt from the side garden and disappear up the back hill. She eased Courtney's head from her lap, managing to get out of the car without waking either of the children. She went up.

Please be home, Joan. Please.

12:30 A.M.

Jack lay quietly now on the bed, but his mind ran like a river, curving, dropping, though not without destination. His thoughts flowed in a single direction, and he knew it wouldn't be long before his entire existence would meet the cataract and fall into the sea. For a while he believed he was a spirit, and wondered what kind of spirit he was. Whatever it was, it had entered through the feet and crawled up to the brain like some deadly African worm waiting to bore into the capillaries and be carried by the blood to the lungs. There it would emerge and begin its crawl up through the throat to be finally expelled in a great choking. It was then, precisely then, that the Voice told him this would be the Final Time. When this was clear to him, he showered and got dressed.

From the moment he got into the Seville he had the desire to use the car phone. It wasn't clear to him exactly what he would say, so the Voice told him to take a very thick line of uncut cocaine: it would give him the energy, the alertness he needed. Check list. Yes, he had turned on the house phone monitors, the transmitter; all the necessary equipment. He had seen the signs of her snooping, but he knew he had locked the library cabinet which housed the important electronic machinery the Voice had told him to buy. There had been no other way to reconnoiter and guard against the enemies within the house.

As he drove he wondered: *Where?* He would drive somewhere until he was ready, until he had all the information he needed. *Marjorie, look, I know how you feel. . . .* He was going to continue talking to her. He felt she could probably read his mind, feel his thoughts coming out through the fog, his thoughts finding her. He most wanted her to know he still loved her and the children . . . but at that moment he saw a stain on the seat beside him. He reached out to touch it. It was small and sticky. Not much larger than a thumbnail. *Who made this stain?* And for a long while as he drove he could think only of the stain, which seemed to be growing larger. If Marjorie was there, he would have wanted to hit her because she would say there wasn't any stain. *It IS there. It's getting bigger and it's spilling across the leather, it's seeping down into the custom tufts. And you can't even see that Marjorie! You can't see that stain. Well, if you can't see that stain, I'm going to have to force you. I will force you down on your knees and rub your nose in it. It is like caramel, Marjorie. It is white caramel from my candy-coated apple, and you're going to refuse to discuss it. You're going to try to divert the subject. Well, then, I will have to force you until you do see the stain. You will see it, and this time you will admit . . .*

He reached out to the tape deck, made a blank cassette ready. He switched to record, pressed the counter at zero. This was too important to disappear. If she couldn't hear him, he would play the cassette for her so she wouldn't have to snoop through his things. *Yes, well, I'll tell you, one of the great secrets of our life, Marjorie. You see, dear one, the mystery of our selves is gone. We are both now witnesses to our own fraud. Try painting a scream, Marjorie. You must be like a girl in a waltz and let yourself go. You must dance, and from your laughter arrive at the screams.*

He lifted the phone, signaled for a mobile operator.

"Yes, the Beverly Hills Police. Thank you. *Hello?* Hello? Yes . . . I'd like to speak with Detective Lichteiman, please. Yes, tell him it's Mr. Love. Find him for Mr. Love . . ."

He listened as the switching, the clicking sounds mixed with static. For a moment he felt as though he had flown through the wires into their switchboard, that he was actually electronically mixed with the electricity and the copper. He heard all the proper sounds, for the middle of the night. *Special equipment.* He was in their special equipment being beamed straight to his Lichteiman's home.

Finally, Lichteiman's voice: "Hello? Hello, Mr. Love? This is Detective Lichteiman. Are you there, Mr. Love?"

He was thrilled with Lichteiman's voice. He could hear the whiskey, the decades of smoking.

"Did I wake you, Mr. Lichteiman?"

"No, Love. Where are you?"

"In my car. I'm calling you from my car, Mr. Lichteiman."

"Are you driving?"

He decided not to answer immediately—but Lichteiman's voice continued: "Is there something special you'd like to talk about?"

Static. He heard Lichteiman moving the wire, changing the phone to his other ear.

"Maybe *you'd* like to talk about something," he told Lichteiman. "Perhaps we could talk about how many angels dance on the head of a pin? I guess we all talk to you, don't we Lichteiman? I mean, I'm not the first, am I?"

"I want you to talk to me. I care about you."

"Why do you *care* about me?"

"Well, I think we are probably very much . . . alike, perhaps. I think you need a friend. I'd like to talk about helping you, Love."

"Well, I don't want you to talk about helping me, Lichteiman."

"What would you like to talk about?"

He laughed: "I want to talk about *Claire's Knee.*"

Static. A beat.

"*Claire's Knee,* the movie?"

"You want to know what kind of car I'm driving, don't you?"

"Do you want to tell me?"

"Why don't you guess, Lichteiman?"

"A Rolls?"

"No."

"A Mercedes?"

"No."

"Are you in trouble tonight, Love? Do you want to meet me tonight?"

"Did you get my tape . . . my feet?"

"Yes. I looked at the tape. You need help, Love. Let me help you."

"*No. You* need help, Lichteiman. You need to listen to my car. I know they're taping this, Lichteiman. I know you're listening to my directionals, to my radio, to every traffic sound around me and that you want to hurt me . . ."

"Listen to me, Love—your mind. There's something different in your mind. Something's happened to make your mind . . ."

"Mr. Lichteiman . . ." he started, and he knew he

sounded furious now, like a killer, "I gave them a baby sucking on a breast. I gave them dead birds and animals. King Richard after a hunt. I gave them ladies and gentlemen shooting carp from canoes. I gave them a boy in a period costume and two women embracing."

"Are you a writer?"

He hung up on Lichteiman, deciding he had talked much too long.

Are you laughing, Lichteiman?

He took the phone from its hook again, and pressed the information digits.

"Hello. Mobile operator? I want some information about the processing of my car phone calls— phone calls from my car."

Ring, ring. Static. A voice. Hello?

"Hello, I'm from a studio . . . yes, a studio. Can you tell me whether the police can trace a car phone call? Yes, it's for a story, a novel. And then if the police could trace it, how long would my character's voice have to stay on?"

The operator's voice: "I'm sorry, but I don't know what the procedure for tracing a car phone call is, sir. You'd have to check with the police department."

"Thank you."

He hung up, then back to another mobile operator. Good. "I want the Los Angeles Police Department, please."

"Any particular division?"

"How are they listed?"

"Like Hollywood, downtown."

"Is there a communications division?"

"No, just a general information number."

"Give me that."

He dialed. At last a man's voice. A man would

know. "Hello, yes. I was wondering if you could help me. I was working on a novel . . . I have someone making a phone call to the police from a car phone . . . do you have any technique for tracing the call?"

"Sure."

"Is it anything like in the Army when they do those signal things. I don't have any idea how they do it."

"I don't know the specifics . . ."

"Could you connect me with the department that *does* know? But you think they could find the car, find which way the car was moving? Yes, but they would need some time. I understand that. Yes, time."

"What area are you in?"

"Beverly Hills."

"I would suggest you call West Los Angeles Station on Monday, during the day when they have a full crew on. They'll be able to answer any questions you might have."

"Thank you so much. Goodbye."

"Goodbye."

He was traveling east on Santa Monica Boulevard now, crossing Doheny. By Fairfax he was in tears again. He tried not to notice all the figures hitchhiking, nor the shapes in the black doorways and against telephone poles. Some stretched out on bus stop benches, groups of three and four on corners. Some didn't look older than twelve, certainly not more than fifteen or sixteen. Boy with dyed hair. A few lesbians were illuminated in a coffee shop. The bars were letting out and it was so sad, so sad. At one stoplight he noticed a boy, perhaps fourteen years old, sitting on a gate. He looked tubercular, anemic, putrified with neglect. The boy smiled, and there were dark spaces

between his remaining rotten teeth. His hair was lifeless, as though he was undergoing some terrible leu-
kemia treatment.

He drove further. All the sad boys, most of whom
would be dead before they reached twenty. They
would be found in swimming pools, overdosed, worn
into death by the sodomy of their lives. And everybody—the police, the priests, rabbis, the wealthy—
knew the children were there. Everyone knew they
were there, but no one knew how to stop this destruc-
tion of boyhood. This boyhood dying . . .

PART III

CHAPTER THIRTEEN

Marjorie had been there when Joan and Hal had come close to separating. She would sit with Joan on the benches near the sandbox of Beverly Pre-School and compare notes on movies, bed-wetting, and all the terrible mothers who had their chauffeurs cart their children to school. She remembered Joan confessing that movies had been her whole life as a growing girl. They had been her youth, her childhood.

But what Marjorie most remembered about Joan was the day Joan had called, weeping, begging her to come over. Hal had told her he wasn't sure he loved her anymore. That he was tired of what he called a tit-for-tat marriage. "You don't love me," he had told her. "You're in a horse race with me!"

1:10 A.M.

The door opened. Joan looked momentarily surprised, and Marjorie realized she was still in her nightgown. Then Joan must have seen *emergency* in her eyes; she moved quickly to help. Marjorie carried Danny. Joan scooped Courtney. Back into the house, down the small hallway to the left. Soon the kids were snug and sleeping in with Joan's children. No questions from Joan. After all, appearances just indicated one more divorce in the works. Mother and children fleeing. Conjugal criminality of the husband.

Joan was reassuring, filling the awkward pauses.
"You stay as long as you like . . . it's no trouble. My
husband tried to slap me last month, but I slugged
him. I found out I'm stronger than he is. I throw a
plate of kielbasa at him once a month to keep him in
shape. He's in Gardena for an all-night poker game.
He does that now; he and his business acquaintances,
as he calls them. They line up six bottles of wine and
call it a wine-tasting conference. They all get drunk."

Joan made coffee, and they sat around the breakfast nook in the kitchen. No demand for details. She
let Marjorie tell as much as she cared to; she joked,
tried to comfort. "Yes, husbands; what are we going to
do with them? I took a real-estate course at UCLA.
Hal felt so threatened I thought he'd kill me. I
wouldn't say Hal doesn't try; he made dinner one
night. The guests almost dropped dead from something he called stew, but at least he made an effort. I
think he still screws around outside, but he shapes up
better whenever he *is* home. I mean, I tried everything
to put a little life into our marriage. I even arranged a
clone-head masquerade party last Halloween. He was
not amused. And then the counselor said, 'Look, Mrs.
Barron, stop devoting one hundred percent of your
energy trying to please him. Stop complaining to
your children about him. You need to relax, build up
your health, and not attach so much importance to
your cars and furniture. You should be more indepen-
dent. You could shop more carefully, learn to live
cheaper. Think about public transportation and public schools. Try a wash-and-wear haircut and skip
Rodeo Drive. Learn to think more of yourself. Learn
how to fix a sink, balance your checkbook, tell off a
salesman! Go someplace by yourself. Make a new
friend by yourself . . .'"

As Joan spoke, Marjorie began to think more clearly. Each time Joan offered the guest room Marjorie told her it wouldn't be necessary. As long as Danny and Courtney could stay, that would be fine. There were things Marjorie still had to do. There was school tomorrow. *School? Am I crazy?* The kids needed their uniforms for school. Children were not admitted to school without their uniforms.

She borrowed an old housedress and some shoes. No, Joan—Jack didn't hit me. Somehow, now with the children safe, she really wasn't afraid of physical violence from him.

She would have to call her husband's psychiatrist, Dr. Dorin. She'd get the number from the phone book, and he would tell her what to do. But she had no right to lay it *all* on Joan. Not the shameful symptoms of the illness. She couldn't bring herself to pronounce those; Joan was fine as far as she went, but Marjorie would need someone tougher for the rest of it.

"You're actually going back there tonight?" Joan asked at the door.

"No. But I have to talk to someone. Everything will be fine as long as the kids stay here," Marjorie said. "But don't tell my husband where they are. If for any reason you have to call my house, don't tell him who you are; don't even speak unless I answer the phone."

Then came Joan's sensible barrage of warnings: *You look very frightened; wait till morning; call the police* . . .

Finally, she seemed to read Marjorie's silent plea to please shut up.

"The kids will be fine, Marjorie," Joan promised.

1:45 A.M.

Marjorie drove back to Sunset, then headed east. She needed Carole. She could tell Carole everything and wouldn't have to worry about shocking her. She also wouldn't have to worry about any of it getting back into the mainstream of society, since most people didn't want anything to do with Carole. She thought about calling Carole, using the phone at the corner of Canon and Sunset. It was either that or the one outside the lavatories on Santa Monica Boulevard. Both were dangerous at this hour. Instead, she drove on, turned off Sunset and started the climb into Trusdale. She was surprised to see that the lights were still blazing at Carole's house in the middle of the night.

Carole was drunk when she answered the door. "Whatsa matta? A drink? Vodka? You want some vodka?"

It was as though she had entered a slow-motion dream. Carole, with her dark young man stretched out by the fire in jeans and cowboy boots. Carole in silver three-inch heels, black leather pants, and a white frilly blouse. "There was a party here for Stella—with all her students. And she was talking about Goldberg, the agent, and it was really very perverse . . ."

"Carole, I'm sorry to interrupt . . ."

"Forget it." Carole called into the living room: "Golden thighs, Marjorie and I are going to chat for a while. Don't wander too far away."

Carole went to the kitchen to get some more ice, and they found a corner, a loveseat of shadows. The living room was white and startling through an archway; Marjorie slid out the facts and Carole listened

without shock. Marjorie knew that to Carole the bi-
zarre was the stuff of daily life.

Carole took a drink of her vodka. "I figured your
husband for a pisser, but not into the milk. Did you
ever just try saying, 'Hey Jack, please don't urinate in
the family milk?' or, if you had been very wise, maybe
you could have just bought extra milk and told him
which ones were his and let him urinate his little
heart away." Carole smiled. She took Marjorie's hand.
"Yes, you might say it's a nervous breakdown, but I
don't think he's the only husband that's pissing into
the family milk. They're all pissing into it these days.
Oh, yes, I'm sure there's something wrong in the
brain, all right . . ."

Marjorie poured out her story, all the *whys* of her
bewilderment. Her husband needed *help*.

"I want an answer."

"Well, let me tell you that although I don't think
it's the most depraved thing—to piss into a milk bottle—well, I would say you're in a lot of trouble. I don't
care whether he was pleading for help or not. And
you're worried about whether or not there's something you can do to help him? I wouldn't worry about
him. I think you could just assume that after you left
he'll notice you're gone. I don't think you'd have to go
into it much more than that. Are you afraid he'll say,
'Why did you leave, Marjorie? Because the toast was
burnt?' 'No, it's because you were trying to fuck your
four-year-old daughter.' I don't think you'll have to
discuss that very much. You left because it was time
to leave. I don't think it brooks a great deal of discussion. If he wonders what's wrong, you just tell him."
She reached out and hugged Marjorie.

"You don't think I should feel *anything* but hate
for him?"

"Oh, I think you should feel a great deal of pity for

him, but let him find pity some other place. Marjorie, this is not a *little* strange, what you have described to me. What you described was rather naughty," Carole said, filling her glass with more vodka. "Don't get terribly worried, just let him book any four-year-olds he wants through the talent agencies out here. You don't need to feel compassion. Your husband is very sick. And I smelled it long ago. I don't care if there is something wrong with the brain, if there's a tumor the size of an artichoke."

"I should call his psychiatrist."

"Oh, I *would* call the psychiatrist and say, 'Get the tumor out of his brain.' But I'll tell you one thing he should never get, and that's *visitation rights*. He ain't gonna see your girl on Sunday, I'll tell you that. There's really nothing very complicated about it. You'll have nothing against him, mind you. But no visitation rights unless with armed guards. If you've got two guys with guns—and if he lays a hand on her—he's dead. That might be okay."

"What if I could do something that would—"

"Marjorie, your suppositions are extraordinary. Ah, he was pleading with you, those great big dark eyes, crying for you as he was saying 'Help me! Help me!' No, Marjorie, *no*. Let him get one of those inflatable dolls and that's it."

"He didn't actually *do* anything to her. He—"

"Marjorie, you will never go back to him. You are never going to redeem him. You will never be able to trust him. It's over, kaput! And the only reason you will be going back now is to secure everything of any value that you possibly can. And when I say now, I mean right this minute. You have jewels, silver, clothes, a mink, and a Cuisinart. And we do that *now*. *He's* the one that gets out. He's the one that deserves the pain."

Carole was on her feet, moving with short rapid steps toward the living room.

"We'll take two cars," Carole insisted. "If he's in a real snit we'll at least have plenty of room to load your stuff."

1:50 A.M.

Jack stopped at Rand's, near the corner of Wilshire and Westwood, opposite the movie complex. The reality of being hungry: a special burger smothered in fried onions, cheese, ketchup. A cockroach crawled up the wall near him. There were a few old people, lonely-looking people from retirement apartments popping bread into individual toasters on their tables, and sipping their insomniac's tea. A woman next to him, someone who looked like she had just escaped from Bedlam, was drinking plain hot water. He ate his burger in silence, and when he had finished he ordered a coffee to go and sipped it as he walked down the dark alley to the parking lot where he had parked the Seville. The Westwood cemetery bordered on the parking lot, and he knew less than thirty feet from him was the chamber that held Marilyn Monroe and hundreds of other corpses stacked one on top of each other in this necropolis behind the movie complex. A memory flickered briefly in his mind. He had gone to Forest Lawn, with its crypts beneath the Hall of the Resurrection. Curtains opening, recorded music; the vision of a stained-glass version of the Last Supper. *Hello, guard, yes, we're coming in here . . .*

2:15 A.M.

Marjorie followed Carole's Mercedes up Loma Vista and down onto Coldwater. She had the Mercedes' top off, said it was in the trunk and she'd only put it on if it rained. Carole's boyfriend was too stoned to come at all.

By the time they arrived at the house, fog completely shrouded Valley Road. Marjorie was thankful to see the Seville was gone. She heard Sam and Sandy barking in the back yard.

"You bet the son-of-a-bitch cleared out," Carole said. Leading the way, she barged in through the unlocked side door. They checked the rooms, the closets, even the back yard. The house *was* empty.

Marjorie let the dogs into the house. She decided that although they'd chew the place to pieces, she needed the protection. Marjorie got the psychiatrist's phone number from the Rollodex in the library. She dialed, knowing she'd only get the answering service.

"This is Dr. Dorin's service. Is this an emergency, ma'am? It's two o'clock in the morning."

"Well yes it *is* an emergency. My husband is one of his patients. We've had some trouble. I need to speak to Doctor Dorin. No, it can't wait until morning. *But, I'm telling you, this is an emergency* . . ."

Carole grabbed the phone from Marjorie's hand. "Now look, you cretins, call that doctor *now*. We are sitting here waiting at 276-9059. You call him and tell him Jack Krenner has fucking flipped out, and unless he wants a good-sized lawsuit up his ass, to get right back to us immediately!"

Carole hung up and headed for the bar. "I hope you've got some Stolichnaya."

"I'll get the children's clothes together."

"Oh, now, wait an itty-bitty minute," Carole ordered. "What you do now is pack *his* clothes, throw them in a box and stick them out in front. In the morning we go pick up the kids and move them back in here along with a couple of Studio City guards and a half-dozen Dobermans." She found the vodka and ice, and poured herself a drink.

"He was never violent. When he was in with Courtney he was begging, pleading. She was crying because of fear, not because he was actually *hurting* her. I don't think he would really hurt his own children."

"Marjorie, you don't owe him anything. You get him institutionalized. You get him put away. Where's your *maid*?"

"She's off."

"No more she's not. Call her now. Tell her to drive her butt right back here. No more days off until we get Pinkerton or whoever the hell we've got to get. And when we've got him behind some very tall link fence with barbed wire and pumped full of Thorazine, then maybe you can say he's not violent."

2:30 A.M.

He had no sooner gotten into the car and started the engine when the light on his transmitter phone flashed—someone was using the phone at home. He lifted the receiver and listened. He was glad to hear Marjorie's voice, glad that she was back at the house. He needed to know where she was, wondered if the children were still with her—because he wanted to take care of it all soon. And then he heard the voice in the background, another woman. He heard her come on the phone. Heard her strident ugliness, her drunken braying at Dr. Dorin's answering service. He had known the sensation of hate in his body when near other women like this one. He knew when such a woman was walking near him, or even looking at him. And sometimes, when Marjorie became unpleasant, he knew the same sensation.

The call ended and the light on his receiver winked out. He had better start heading back. There was so much work to do.

Doctor Dorin called back within ten minutes. Marjorie began to tell him what Jack had done, what had happened. She was breaking down as she began to pour it onto him, and he had to interrupt her three times before she finally understood what he was saying.

"Mrs. Krenner, *your husband only came to me for three visits.*"

"He told me he was seeing you three times a week."

"Mrs. Krenner, I haven't seen your husband in more than a month."

"Dr. Dorin, I don't know what to do. Could you please tell me what I should do?"

Carole was alert now. Her eyes were locked into Marjorie's. She took another sip of vodka. Marjorie stuttered now. "But Dr. Dorin, you *did* talk to him. Dr. Dorin, his *problem.* You have to know his *problem.* I understand the professional relationship, but you don't understand what *he tried to do to our daughter!*"

Carole grabbed the phone, "Look doctor, this is a friend of Mrs. Krenner's and she's very upset. We know her husband has serious problems, so don't give us any of this failure to disclose. Now you met three times with that looney—you know what the hell's wrong with him, or you have a damn good idea, and you'd better tell us."

Marjorie tried to take the phone back, but Carole wouldn't let her. She held on tightly, switching gears, trying to sound pleasant. "Now look, doctor, he's never beaten her or the children, doctor, I'm telling you it is *not* a personal problem between a man and a wife, there is nothing personal about it any more. . . . Yes, she is going to want to prefer charges. I know it's her goddamn privilege, and I know it's her right, and I know it's her business! Now look, you son-of-a-bitch, you'd just better care if she prefers charges or not. Because I think that man is very, very sick and I don't have all your degrees and training and experience listening to bullshit. All I'm asking you to do is tell us whether we have to be ready to cut his balls off if he comes back here. Am I getting through to you, Doctor Dorin?"

2:40 A.M.

Jack had the phone resting comfortably on his right shoulder, listening to the ugly, ugly lady's voice as he turned off Sunset onto Roxbury. Very unpleasant.

On the right was Jimmy Stewart's home. He always thought that was one of the nicest homes in the flats. It certainly had the most land, the magnificent corner plot next to his home filled with nothing but trees and flowers, gorgeous flowering shrubs; the autumn coolness had swollen the azalea buds to bursting. *Oh yes, there used to be a house there on the corner and that guy had a tree and the leaves used to fall into Jimmy's pool, so Jimmy didn't like it. And Jimmy asked the guy if he could trim his tree so the leaves wouldn't fall into his pool, but the guy said, "No, up yours, Jimmy." And so when the guy's house went up for sale Jimmy bought it and knocked down the house and put in a flower garden. See, so now Jimmy doesn't have to worry about any more leaves in his pool . . . and . . .*

Ugly woman . . .

Ugly . . .

The lady's voice had hurt his ears very much as he began the climb into the hills.

2:50 A.M.

"You need coffee. I need more vodka."

Carole the mongoose—the image slid quickly into Marjorie's mind. The mongoose, always ready to attack any husband viper.

Carole had lit a fire of large eucalyptus logs in the den fireplace; she curled herself up in front of it. "You know Grugman's wife," she went on, "the real estate guy. He wanted to stay in the house, but we put *him* out. That was the only other wife I ever knew who thought about getting out. He's the guilty one, not you. You sleep in the nice comfortable bed; let him go to a hotel. He'll be lucky if he doesn't have to bed down on a pea farm."

"I don't think I should have come back here," Marjorie said.

"Are you kidding? If that sister Bernice of his smelled divorce she'd be in here on the first morning plane. She'd get in here and suck up everything she could get her hands on."

"I don't care about my *stuff*. I care about my kids. I must be completely crazed because what I'm worried about now are their school uniforms," Marjorie had to laugh. "I'm worried about all the things they're going to need . . ."

"You stay here and don't worry about any of that. If you feel better with the kids out of here for a couple of weeks until they do a lobotomy or whatever the hell they've got to do to him—"

"I'm frightened, Carole."

"Look, did he go after you with a gun? I mean did he try to choke Courtney?"

"No."

"When I squared off against him at the party, I want to tell you, he was shaking inside. I could see right through him. He's probably out of the state by now."

"But you don't know that. He could be doing anything. I don't know."

"If you clear out you're giving up the right to everything in the house . . ."

"I don't want to stay in the house. Something tells me I shouldn't."

"*Why not?* Why shouldn't you stay here? Honey, I've got a sawed-off shotgun up the street. If he comes back here I'll blow his legs off."

"Joan would let me stay at her house. I could stay there with the kids."

"Honey, are you kidding? You'd go from fifty-four hundred square feet to somebody's guest room? I've heard of cruel and unnatural punishment, but you're taking the cake. This is *your* home. He doesn't deserve this home any more. He's lost his rights. Tomorrow we'll turn it into a goddamn fort until he's arrested or whatever the hell happens to him. You gotta press charges, you gotta. You're not the criminal. It's not your fault. You haven't done anything wrong—why should you be running?" Carole gave Marjorie another hug, and for a moment Carole's real concern flickered in her eyes.

The water started to boil, and Carole followed

Marjorie into the kitchen. Marjorie took a tea bag and dipped it several times into a cup of the hot water.

"You really oughta get an automatic hot tap. I gotta call Joey, okay?" Carole wheezed.

"Sure."

Carole hunched over the fluorescent-lit kitchen desk and dialed, while Marjorie strolled back into the den. She found herself staring at the family portrait gallery. The Krenners in Athens; the Krenners in Moscow, the Krenners *everywhere*, it seemed. The photos ended at two large silver framed posters of calla lillies which they brought with them from New York. She began to remember the other, gentler memories of her husband. Jack Krenner, the good husband, the good father. More pictures, memories. Jack holding baby Danny in front of the Church of the Sacred Blood in Leningrad. Jack and Marjorie covered with Tahitian frangipani leis. Jack and Marjorie on the reef with Bora Bora in the background. *Doing* things together. Good times. Jack with Courtney and Danny in front of the Acropolis. If he got well, perhaps they could go back to the way they were. *He didn't go crazy by himself.*

CHAPTER FOURTEEN

3:00 A.M.

Jack pulled the Seville into a dark cul de sac off Loma Vista. The light on the car telephone had come on, signaling someone was on the house phone again. He lifted the phone carefully, listened to a woman's voice. It wasn't Marjorie. Another moment. Yes, the ugly lady, talking to a stoned young man. Drunk Carole in his home. Drunk Carole saying she cannot leave. *"Look, she's my best friend, and her husband's a real sicko.* I mean, she's a lovely sweet girl, lovely children. She's married to this . . ."* Drunk Carole whispering, whispering into the phone to her young man. *"Honey, I can't leave.* I've got to stay here. She's scared. There's a real *piece* of that guy missing."

Jack listened, and an invective began to form in his throat. He tried pronouncing the word, this curse inspired by the lady's voice. An invective toward that woman in his home, saying things to his wife, telling his wife things about him, telling this man about him. The phrase. The word became a phrase. *Oh, when you feel that something isn't coming out, what you've got to do is put your word, put your FUCK into jibberish. You make a sound. You don't say the word, you make the sound . . .*

He covered the mouthpiece, shaking as the sound began to form. Finally, the noise he was making in his car was so violent he had to hang up the receiver. He started driving again, down the hill toward Sunset. When the light went off he knew the bad woman was gone. He lifted the receiver again. The mobile operator, then the cop on the switchboard. Finally, Lichteiman's voice.

"Hello?"

"You said you wanted to talk about *helping* me? Did I wake you up?"

"No. I would like to talk . . ."

"You sound drunk, Lichteiman."

"I *am* drunk. Are you on drugs? You sound stoned, Love."

"Are they tracing my call?"

"No."

"They *can't* trace my call."

"Are you driving?"

"Yes. I'm at the corner of Rexford and Loma Vista now. But I'm moving and you can't find me."

"What are you thinking, Love?"

"I'm thinking about visiting a producer. I'm thinking about stopping by my producer's house and telling him about a new idea I have."

"What kind of an idea?"

"It's a television idea. This producer thinks he's feature, but he's really television, and I heard he's had his jaw wired so that he'll lose weight, and that he's in his kitchen putting pizzas into a blender so he can fit them past the wires, drink the pizzas past the wires . . ."

"Do you want to hurt him, Love?"

"I want to tell him a story, pitch a story about a wife and husband . . . *different* . . . and now I see why the husband's affected, the reason he's beginning to get affected by this image, these images . . . is because he's surrounded . . . it's like Monopoly . . . and he almost thinks it's real, Lichteiman. He almost think's it's real . . ."

"What's real, Love?"

"And we can use this . . . show . . . play it against what we're all suffering, and every week we can have a new economic problem, all the things we're all pressured by . . . I'd like to tell her . . ."

"*Her?*"

"The *her* producer with his jaws wired, and drinking the pizzas . . . and I have an axe in the trunk . . ."

A *clink*!

"Lichteiman, what was that noise?"

"I'm drinking. Sorry, my glass hit the mouthpiece."

"I'm going by Thrifty's now. I'm in a new zone . . ."

"I can't trace you, Love."

"My sister sent me the final bill for the headstone . . . my mother's headstone . . . and I had a dream. I dreamed I laid out all my clothes on my bed but I did not die . . . I had to use a few sensory words, I use sensory words like *clearly* and *quiet* . . . I like saying those because when I say them I feel good . . . good in the hallucinations . . ."

"You have hallucinations, Love?"

"Other people think I do, but I don't. They think I act as though I am reliving shock treatments . . ."

"You've had shock treatments?"

"In my dreams, I dreamed my sister and I were reading a magazine and I wanted my mother to see something and I stuck the magazine into her eye and they had to give me shock treatments . . ."

"Do you dream a lot, Love?"

"*Fuck you.*"

"Why did you say that, Love?"

"You only want to catch me, you fucker."

"Love, I'm too pissed to catch anyone tonight. Can't you hear I'm pissed?"

Laughter. Hysterical laughter.

Then:

"I'm very depressed, Lichteiman."

"Let me help, Love . . ."

"Please help me . . ."

"Are you going to hurt anyone tonight?"

"No."

"Are you sure?"

"Not unless the Voice tells me . . ."

"What has the Voice been saying, Love?"

"It's playing games. It's been lying to me."

"Like what?"

"The Voice told me to kill myself."

"What did the Voice say?"

"What I want you to know, Lichteiman, is that I'm not a stupid man. I'm very bright. I'm very sensitive. I feel things in the world, and voices speak to me. They teach me things that scientists don't understand until years later. And so, Lichteiman, I guess what I really want from you is to tell me, how do I get my *face* back? I've lost my face again. I don't want to do it, but I'm going to do it. I have a glimpse into the dynamics of my flaw, Lichteiman. I have wonderful characters. I write wonderful spirits. I have very high payoffs for all of my characters that I write about. And I know there is a character inside of me that is going to do a very horrible, horrible thing that I would never do in my lifetime. I don't want to do it, but I have to . . . I have this thing that's *missing*, Lichteiman. I'm missing some element of emotion. Some pigment is missing from my palette of colors. If I could only have that piece, I could go straight to the head of the class."

"Are you missing a sense of humanity, Love?"

"If you could just tell me . . ."

"But aren't you aware of it all? Don't you really have a sense of what's missing from you? Isn't what you want a sense of *oneness*?"

"Oneness . . ."

"And you want to know how to achieve *oneness.*"

"Yes, I think that's what I want to achieve. What is stopping me now, Lichteiman?"

"Well, I'd guess it has to do with a tremendous vulnerability that you must feel. Your vulnerability has probably always stopped you from feeling the fullness you need for other people. Are you hung up on defending yourself, Love? Are you finally tired of defending, lashing out, because if you are, Love, that's called the first sign of growing up. Are you growing up, Love? Because when you are grown up you will not be afraid anymore. You *are* still afraid of people. You lash out because of fear. And I'm sure the voice inside you is the voice of fear."

"People think what I write is hateful."

"But you're not hateful, are you, Love?"

"No."

"You weren't treated so good as a kid, were you, Love?"

"I was mutilated, Lichteiman. Mutilated as a kid."

"Have you ever written about a hero?"

"No. . . . Someone's using the phone again at my house. I have to hang up. I'll call you tomorrow."

"It is tomorrow. *How do you know someone's using your phone?*"

Jack hung up and switched the receiver over to pick up the call.

3:15 A.M.

Carole had curled back up in front of the roaring fire in the den and was still going strong on the Stolichnaya. "I've got some grass at the house. Do you want me to run up and get you some?" she asked Marjorie. "You look like you could do with a good joint."

"No. I'm fine." And for the moment she was being quite truthful. Her strongest anxiety now concerned the children. *Are they sleeping? Are they having nightmares? Courtney coughing, choking, beginning one of her pre-asthmatic syndromes?* Why hadn't she thought to grab the medicine? She could have at least remembered the Sudafed. But Joan probably had some in her own medicine cabinet. She thought about calling Joan, but remembered all the taping equipment in the library. Everything she and Carole had said—or would say—on the phone might be going onto a cassette someplace. And if Jack did come back, he would listen to the cassettes and become very angry. He would be very, very angry if he heard what Carole had said. If she dialed Joan he'd probably even know where the children were. He'd be able to listen to the sound of the dial beeps and could tell which digits she had pressed, if he was as electronically proficient as she now suspected he was. She thought about going to the library and ripping out all the recorders and wires, but she might destroy the phone connection. She'd have the company send a repair man in the morning and . . .

Ringgg.
Ringgggg!
"Jesus Christ, who could this be?" Carole brayed.
Marjorie lifted the receiver.

"Hello."

"Hello, Marjorie, it's Joan. I don't want to worry you, but . . ."

"Is Courtney breathing funny?"

"No. She's breathing fine, but she's crying, screaming. She says she can't go to sleep without her Binky teddy bear. She's throwing a fit. I told her she could have Jake's lion, and Jenny has a raccoon, but she says she's not going to stop screaming until she has her Binky. I don't want her working herself into—"

"Mommy, I want Binky! I can't sleep without Binky! Where are you, Mommy?"

The sound of Courtney crying returned Marjorie to the nightmare. Her poor girl frightened in a strange house and strange bed. "Honey, I'll bring Binky over in the morning. All right, honey? You go to sleep, get some sleep. Ask Joan to let you have one of Jenny's stuffed animals."

"I want my Binky, Mommy! I want Binky! I want him! Mommy, I'm having *bad dreams.* I'm having *bad dreams,* Mommy. *Where are you, Mommy?"*

"All right, honey. Please don't be scared. Everything's going to be fine, dear. Put Joan on."

"I love you, Mommy. Please bring Binky."

"I love you too, Court. Just put Joan on. I'll bring your Binky. Binky's coming," she found herself saying.

"Hi, Marjorie?"

"Joan, I'll bring their things over now."

Joan's voice slid into a whisper: "Marjorie, don't make the trip for that. She's heard your voice. She knows everything is fine. She can just use one of the other animals. I feel stupid bothering you, but she needed some kind of assurance, needed to hear your voice."

"I want to drop off some medicine for Courtney, some Theodur and Alupent in case she slips into even the slightest asthmatic breathing. It usually comes on over several hours, but if you notice her coughing, you can start the medication. It avoids a full attack."

"She's quieted down, Marjorie. I think it could just wait until morning."

"I'll be right there."

Marjorie hung up and rushed to fill a plastic shopping bag with the medicines, the supplies. Toothbrushes, clothes, chew vitamins.

"Look, she said they were all right," Carole reminded her. "Don't bother going over there now. If you give in, you just spoil them. She told you she'll sleep fine."

"You could drive over with me, Carole."

She looked at Carole and realized Carole really wasn't going anywhere. The alcohol had obviously taken its toll, relaxing her face into a mask of complete exhaustion.

"You could drive over with me, Carole."

"I just built the fire," Carole moaned. "We have the fire going. What are we going to do, put it out?"

"Well, I'm sorry, if you were a mother you would understand, Carole."

"You're being compulsive, Marjorie."

"I don't care whether it's compulsive or whether it isn't. I'm just telling you I'm not going to get any rest until my daughter has her medicine."

"Look, where the hell is your maid?" Carole rasped. "You didn't call her, did you?"

"I'm not going to wake her up."

"Look, what the hell are these overpaid aliens for if they can't help out once in a while?" Carole slurred. Then she swallowed the rest of her vodka and headed for the kitchen phone. "I'll get her ass over here . . ."

3:20 A.M.

Jack decided to park the Seville at the end of the Loonridge development. He knew Lichteiman would be coming for him, closing, so he would abandon the car very soon. He knew they could have used transmitters, or perhaps a homing device had been hidden in his car when the dealer had last serviced it. The young mechanic had seemed strange, snooping and overly friendly. Yes, he was the kind of mechanic who bugs cars. Or perhaps in his conversations with Lichteiman he could have mentioned *Climatrol* or *Information Panel*, some slight slip that could have signaled even in the first call what kind of car he was driving. Lichteiman could have heard the signal light—it could be a special sound. Or the phone company could have located his zone, or even his number and then provided the make of the car. He didn't *really* know. And he had auditioned enough actors in his lifetime to smell that Lichteiman's concentration wasn't totally on him. Lichteiman was doing *something*. But even if they found the car, they wouldn't be able to focus in on the house. There wasn't really enough time for Lichteiman to have his address. Not his home. His *home*. Besides, now he could walk there and do what had to be done.

He was about the leave the car when the transmitter light signaled another call in progress. He lifted the receiver, tried to control his breathing. He heard Marjorie's voice. Marjorie and . . . a woman . . . talking about his children. *Joan.* And, yes, the children. Joan *who*? Oh, a Joan with her young Jake. His Courtney with a Jenny? No, it wasn't one of the usual houses, it wasn't anyone from the car pool. Marjorie was talking to a carefully selected Joan. *A Joan to keep my children away from me.* This was a Joan he knew Marjorie wanted him never to think of. A Joan with children, and it was too early in the school year to bring children in the middle of the night to any new Joan from the new school. This would have to be an *old* Joan. This would have to be a mother from the Beverly Pre-School or the park—or a teacher. This had to have been a *Joan* Marjorie had mentioned, unless there were two Joans. He remembered one was a song writer, or said she was a song writer, dressed in suede, dirty suede, foul suede. A dirty suede mother and a profligate father who lived like pigs in a stilt house off Tower. No, not *that* Joan. That was not Marjorie's Joan. It would be another Joan. The Joan and *Hal* from New York. Bel Air. Fourth of July. Six or seven couples with kids—and one of the little kids, a boy, slipped off the edge of the deep end, and going under—his father racing, diving into the pool, pulling him out. The kid frightened, screaming, gasping at an unforgettable Fourth of July event. That remote, distant, pretty Joan. That was Marjorie's Joan.

He would wait in the car. He would wait until Marjorie had packed the children's things, the medicine. He would wait to see if Carole went with her. And while he waited he would feel safe, like an owl high on Loonridge looking down on the dark little hamlet of Lost Orchard. If any car did drive onto Loonridge, he could easily slip out of the car and disappear into the jungle of the canyon.

3:30 A.M.

It was less than an hour before Lichteiman got the call telling him that the Hollywood Division could make the surveillance vans available—with possibly a third van coming in from West L.A. He had spent the time getting dressed and finishing off the Korbel. Finally, he selected his weapons. A .22-caliber pistol which he liked to carry in his jacket. A magnum for the special occasions when he needed the kind of power that could penetrate an engine block. As an afterthought he removed a telescopic rifle from the trunk and laid it on the front seat. He didn't know quite why. He rarely used a rifle, except for rural pursuits. He'd actually had only one occasion to use it— in a small town when he'd come across a dying horse that had been hit by a truck on the highway just outside of Mazatlan. He had enjoyed several vacations in Mexico, enjoyed the mysteries in its Indians and mountains. He once chatted with the equivalent of a very local sheriff: "Oh, we no shoot men here, we don't kill our killers. No corporal punishment," one of the sheriffs had told him in broken English. "No, like we got a jail man now and he kill a witch, and other people. We not kill our killers, señor. It is against our beliefs to kill hombres . . ."

"What do you do, just keep them in jail?" Lichteiman had asked.

"We let man go. We drive man to edge of town where no roads and point to mountains. Man run to mountains, then we go back to town put up the notice terrible beast, míra—terrible animal at the end of town and heading for mountains. This is *beast*, not man. *Then we all take guns and go kill beast . . .*"

3:35 A.M.

Carole was very pleased with the way she handled Maria. It required a very special talent to properly persecute Spanish maids. She had had twenty or thirty working for her at different times over the years. They had come and gone but she knew every trick in their bags, whether they came from Guadala-jara, Guatemala, or Colombia.

"Hello, who *eees* this?"

"Is this Maria?"

"Hello, who *eees* this?"

"I'll tell you who this is. I'm calling for Marjorie Krenner, and we want you over here on the double. *Comprende?* Mrs. Krenner is not here. She just left, but she'll be back!"

Carole fixed herself another drink and found herself slipping into regret. She'd only had sex with one of her houseboys. That was *Jesús,* and she'd only tried him out because the matron she'd stolen him from said he had talents beyond the *jardín.* But now Carole only hoped that Maria would get to the house before Marjorie got back. She knew Marjorie didn't have the right strength to shape up her help. Carole would enjoy that part of it very much. There was no paper lining on the kitchen shelves. There was silver to be polished. The wine glasses were stored inappropriately, dangerously. *Now I want you to have this silver counted for Mrs. Krenner. I don't want to see a single fork or spoon missing. This goes for the stainless steel as well as the silver platters. Maria, you've been cutting your hours shorter. You're just like all the other Marias in this town. And Maria, if you ever do get another day off, I don't want to see you carrying bags or suitcases or anything else filled with Marjorie's soap powder, blueing agents or powdered bleach. I told Marjorie to start counting the cans of tuna fish, crab meat, and especially lobster. I don't want you to remove so much as a single packet of Lipton's Cup-O-Soup. I know you're not stupid enough to take jewelry or furs, but I know, you little dear, you know the value of Steuben glassware. If there is any Steuben missing, we're going to squeal on you. That goes for Wedgwood, Baccarat,*

Corning Ware, and Pottery Barn. If there is so much as a penny or lipstick missing from my bag, you will be on the first van south of the border. Do I make myself clear?

Maria arrived within the hour, but by then Carole was too drunk to give the lecture.

"You just wait for the señora. I need to go to *mi casa* for a *momentita*," Carole told her. "I need a little pick-me-up. If Marjorie comes back before me, just tell her I'll be right there. *Adios, chiquita.* And stop looking at me like I'm *borracho.*"

3:50 A.M.

Carole told herself she'd just go back to her house, roll a couple of joints and come back. She'd have to come back, or Marjorie wouldn't talk to her again. She freshened up her drink and carried it with her out to the car.

The Mercedes started, then stalled in the night fog. She turned the ignition on again while tapping the accelerator—and the motor began to hum. She let it warm up for a minute, shifted and started to move back up Valley Road. She drove carefully over the "slow-down" bumps in the road, and finally pulled her car up to the stop sign. She turned her head sharply to the left to see if any traffic was speeding around the curve on Coldwater. She had learned a long time ago that she needed the visibility of the convertible to compensate for her drinking. The left was clear, but before she could straighten her head or instruct her foot to press the accelerator, she saw a shadow flying toward her. A moment later the dark form leapt into the car with her. Her first stunned thought was that it was a bear, a large beast, but now there were human hands and arms crushing into her. Instantly, her reflexes took over. She had always been remarkable in an emergency, even when drunk. She slammed her foot down on the accelerator, and instead of bolting down Coldwater, she twisted the wheel left and created a surge of centrifugal force that pulled him from her. But he was still in the convertible. Recovering from the unexpected motion, he locked his hands around her throat again. Carole felt her skin about to rip, and this time she swung the wheel to the right and rushed the car over an embankment. She braced herself for the dead stop, and he was thrown from her once more. She opened the door and was out, running back up the shoulder to the road. She started to run down Coldwater. She was screaming now. There would have to be a car. *A car would come, a car would have to come.*

She was a good distance down the road before she dared glance behind her. She prayed that he had been knocked unconscious or killed, that his skull had hit the windshield with enough force to shatter it. *There would have to be a car.*

She was looking in front of her now, eyes watching for any treacherous branch or stone. Then, without turning, she realized he was quite alive. She could hear him running after her. She listened carefully to her footfalls, and his. His were an echo off the canyon wall, then a sound closer behind her. She remembered his hands on her, the strong, thick fingers and his watch that scraped and raked her skin. She heard a sobbing, a crying from behind her. In front of her the canyon fell only deeper into the blackness of the fogroad. But there on the right, down the slope: a light. Someone lived there. Someone was home. But the driveway was too far ahead. She would have to cut through the brush and trees. She started to scramble down the embankment. Her legs were fighting, pulling her torso through the high grass and desert bush.

A wild glance behind her: he was still coming, a monstrous image, weeping. Weeping angrily. He was lunging toward her now, throwing himself against the branches of an overgrown orchard of lemon trees. There was the smell of fern and pine. She heard him crashing closer, much closer.

She struggled to retain her balance as her skirt caught on a branch, tearing, nearly knocking her down. The monster was nearer. And now it was fright itself that made her fall. This time when she came up, long branches yanked at her hair and drove cruelly into her face. She lifted her arms in front of her, screaming, running blind. And now *she* was crying. He was so close now she could feel his hot, sweating aura at her back. She looked over her shoulder once more and a branch stabbed through her leather slacks, nearly piercing her thigh, scratching across her stomach like an animal's claw. She would have to not *feel* the pain until she reached the house. The door would open. There would be a family waiting to save her. A mother and father and young strong boy, a lover to save her from the attacking madman.

Then suddenly she felt the tremendous weight. His body rolled onto her, his feet literally trying to climb the back of her legs until she went down. He was on top of her, turning her over. *Scream*, she told herself. *Scream*, louder and louder. Her lungs shivered and crashed against the weight of his body. He would punch her in the jaw, perhaps break a few ribs. He would knock her out, *even fuck her*, and then she could awaken as she had when other men had beaten her. Even as she lost consciousness with his fingers digging into her throat she believed that she would live . . .

CHAPTER FIFTEEN

4:00 A.M.

Lieutenant Levon was waiting for Lichteiman in front of the station with the Special Forces vans and crews. They had to be borrowed from LAPD, but it was not the first time Lichteiman had used them. And it was not their first emergency response. Lichteiman would call the shots, but Levon would handle his men. The two trucks were equipped to pick up any call Love would make within a twenty-mile radius. Van Alpha, with Levon, would remain in the Rexford and Santa Monica area. Van Beta was to be moved to Wilshire and Beverly Glen. Levon and his crew in van Alpha would process the reception reports and, if they were lucky, plot the location of primal transmission.

"Like World War II," Straub had muttered.

Lichteiman made no comment. He was not a big fan of Straub or Levon. Levon had been helpful in the past, but was too anal. Never bent a rule. Police professionalism with a vengeance.

"A lot of ketchup on this pizza, huh?" Levon grinned. He was as old as Lichteiman, but thin, hard as hickory. Lichteiman envied his energy, but Levon envied Lichteiman's celebrity. In the fluorescence of the detective pool, Levon looked more like a typewriter salesman than a police electronics specialist.

Eyes that moved too quickly to drink in every motion. *A real fuck*, Lichteiman thought, *but he'll do a good job.*

"How long do you want the vans in position?" Straub asked.

"Until I tell you otherwise."

"Still a joy to work with, aren't you Lichteiman?"

Now, the wait.

The wait for Love to call. And Lichteiman knew the call was coming. He had a good nose for smelling both madness and endings.

4:01 A.M.

Jack drove slowly along Sunset, listening to one of the late-night talk shows on the radio. Someone by the name of Mrs. Fox had called in to share a success story: "I just wanted to let your listeners know that I agree with the grandfather who was looking for something worthwhile to do with his life. I was also a secretary and I'm seventy-three years old today. I wanted all your listeners to know that I went to a workshop at UCLA in order to help me change my career. I found it thrilling, and I know there are a lot of people who could benefit from that particular workshop. It did more for me in one day than years of counseling."

"Tell me how it changed your life," the interviewer urged in her soft voice.

"It just gave me a feeling of tremendous self-worth and usefulness. The kind of feeling I haven't had in years."

"How did you regain that feeling?"

"Well, the man who ran the workshop got us to list verbs, a whole series of verbs about things that we could do. Verbs like 'organizing,' 'teaching,' 'helping,' 'loving.' This man gave us verbs which just gave me the confidence to try to go on and not feel as totally discounted by society as I have . . ."

And then the commercials, followed by more commercials. American selling on the radio. *And here's Lloyd Bridges with a message for all pool owners. "Would you like to have chlorine that lasts twice as long? . . . And here's the good news, if you act immediately, you can get one-and-a-half pounds of free chlorine packed in with every twenty-pound pail of Sun Chlorine granules." And now here is Bob "Cal Fed" Hope: "Everybody dreams of retiring with a nest egg, but dreaming about it won't make it happen. That's why it's never too early to open up a new IRA account at California Federal Savings.*

". . . For a family on the way up this policy can guarantee the survival of a young business and avoid problems in the event of a principal's untimely death . . ."

He had to stop for a light at Beverly Glen.

Marionettes.

He remembered his childhood marionettes.

Nautical, laughing, demoniacal. Some he had made himself. One, a grotesque sailor, was given to him for his second birthday. He recalled cardboard boxes which he had turned into dioramas, crepe-paper palm trees backlighted by flashlight bulbs attached with twisted paperclips. And the aquariums. He had two one-gallon, a five-gallon, and a twenty-gallon tank. And he would sit for hours looking at guppies hunting their young in the forests of elodea. And that strange event that occurred to him when he was just starting out. He was walking through Greenwich Village with a friend, and they went to see *The American Dream* at the Cherry Lane Theatre. After the show, about two hours later, they were back out on the street. Suddenly his friend began to run. He ran, crying out, "Something's going on in the alley."

The alley was several blocks away, and Jack ran after his friend thinking it was just a lot of fun and nonsense. But when he reached the alley, he saw people hanging out their windows, yelling and throwing coins and dollar bills down to an old woman who was hovering over a row of garbage pails. She was stuffing the garbage into her mouth and ignoring the money as it fell around her. That incident haunted him his entire life, until once he had met a writer and told him about it, and the writer had told him it was not amazing at all. The writer had told him, quietly and simply, that the woman eating the garbage was doing penance.

Beverly Hills is turning into a ghost town. I am simply going down with the town. The complete joke is that we ourselves may not be stars of the greatest magnitude. It's rather deafening, that infinity. What is all this glitter against infinity? And my cruelty, my cruelty is as great as the town, my cruelty of bringing people onto this earth, and giving them dreams. What right did I ever have to give children any dreams at all. Now he had to laugh. For a moment he realized that in a sense he himself had turned into a giant movie machine. He had actually become what he had beheld. But it would be different with him. He had begun to do his own cutting, his own editing. He would stop the machine, turn it off forever. *The great fraud of wealth. The great stifling of the animal in us. They have stopped the animal in me. I needed some of the animal to stay alive. I cannot bear the airways filled with the corruption of Burger King and Disneyland. The constant bombardment to pull the dollars out of our pockets. This town and country completely geared to smile the bucks out of our guts. The liars and the cheaters and the banks with*

*the points, the galloping, spiralling, colossal greed
which is front and foremost in this town. The rats are in
the granaries. The rats are everywhere.*

4:05 A.M.

Joan was waiting for Marjorie as she came up the
front walk. "They're all asleep. I'm really sorry I both-
ered you, you poor dear. Is that Binky?"

"Yep." Marjorie held aloft the rather ridiculous-
looking teddy in ripped overalls with one button eye
missing. "It doesn't matter. The way things are going,
I don't think I'm going to have to diet after all. That's
the positive side to running around like a crazy
woman."

While Marjorie looked in on the children, Joan
did a nonstop commiseration: "You remember when
Hal and I were having our little sessions? I lost
twenty-three pounds, thinking that would make me
able to blow his socks off. I finally went to a psychic
nutritionist. He diagnosed me as being bulimious.
That's what they call it when a woman feels rebuffed
by her man and devastates her body by developing a
voracious appetite. Can you believe it? Hal's turned
into a computer freak since we used to talk. He's got
this whole house on computers. He's made me put my
grocery list on computer. We've got everything in this
house except possibly nuclear fusion, and he still
bitches at me for not rolling his clean socks into little
balls."

Marjorie appreciated the fact that Joan didn't
push her, pump her for information. She was very
tempted to stay now, to accept her offer of the guest
room, not to go back to the house. But there was Carole. And she was probably passed out by now in front
of the fireplace . . .

"I'll be back in the morning. I'll call you," Marjorie said, "unless there's another problem with the kids. I've been advised not to move out of the house."

"I wouldn't. Don't worry about the kids. They'll be fine now."

"Courtney's breathing sounds good to me," Marjorie said. "What do you think?"

"It's fine, Marjorie. If anything comes up, I'll call you. I promise."

Joan watched Marjorie get in the Volvo and drive off. As Joan closed the front door, she saw something that seemed slightly strange, a car parked farther up the canyon street. She noticed it mainly because its lights went on immediately after Marjorie drove off. Then it began lumbering slowly down the street. A Seville, Joan noted. To her surprise, it swung quickly into her driveway and stopped. In a moment the driver's door was open and a man was walking swiftly, angrily toward her.

CHAPTER SIXTEEN

4:20 A.M.

The call finally came.

"Shut up," Lichteiman roared into the detective pool. The room fell silent. "Check Levon," he ordered, and pressed the flashing button on his extension.

"Hello," Lichteiman said calmly.

There was static, then a clearing. The line was open. The caller wasn't speaking.

"Hello, are you there, Love?" Lichteiman pursued.

Finally:

"Yes, I'm here."

Lichteiman signaled Straub that contact was made, that he could hear Love was driving again. "I was just having a little coffee. What are you doing?"

"Nothing. I was wondering where you live? Are you home, Mr. Lichteiman?"

Lichteiman breathed deeply, nearly yawned to sound conversational. "Yes, I live at the top of the hill. Sky, the sea, trees. It's very nice up here. Do you live with your wife?"

"No."

"Are you home now, Love?"

"No."

There was too long a silence now. Lichteiman continued quickly, "I live alone. I really like being alone. I just like the quiet. I read a lot. Do you ever read?"

Straub stood with four of the Detectives, whispering into a direct-link phone to van Alpha. Lichteiman knew Levon would be making up for Straub's lack of experience. He would only have to stay linked to Love. Make Love believe that they were the only two people in the world.

"Would you like to tell me about your home?" Lichteiman asked. He wouldn't fish for more data about the car.

"No. I want to talk to you about my *soul*."

Lichteiman forced a lightness. "You're probably the only one in this town that even thinks they have a soul anymore."

"I know it's your job to find out who I am."

"You'll tell me when you feel like it."

Lichteiman heard a sound, something guttural, bestial. Then: "You'd like me to just throw up all over the phone to you, wouldn't you? You want to know where I am."

"Only if you want to tell me."

Levon's voice, muted from a walkie-talkie: "Van Alpha has signal. Van Beta scanning. Three cars at Sunset and Doheny. Two cars Mulholland and Dixie Canyon. Now van Beta has signal. Signal in motion. Suspect driving car. Suspect in motion . . ."

"*Do you think I'd like to hurt you, Lichteiman?*"

"I don't think so."

"People don't like to lose their . . . enemies."

"Do you think of me as your enemy?"

"Aren't you?"

"No. I could be your friend." (*Innocuous, don't patronize, connect, do double-time to connect, emotionally involve him.*) "Your wife and children. I'm sure they're your friends. I'm sure you love them."

Levon's voice, excited: "Van Alpha projecting vehicle to be approaching Coldwater from Laurel Canyon. Expect to sight vehicle . . ."

"I haven't been able to feel anything, Mr. Lichteiman. *Yes, I am a writer, Mr. Lichteiman. I was a
writer . . .*"

"Do you work in the movies, Love?"

"I build pyramids."

"Pyramids like in Egypt."

"No, celluloid pyramids. The kind like Barbra
and her hairdresser entomb themselves in."

"And how do you help *build* their pyramids,
Love?"

"I give them visions. They build their pyramids
out of my visions. I give them my images."

LEVON: "Van Beta pinpoints vehicle proceeding down
canyon. Suspect vehicle less than point-two miles.
Interference from racing vehicles on Mulholland.
Suggest block Loma Vista at Cherokee . . ."

"The images you told me about, Love?"

"Others."

"Like what, Love?"

"I gave them the death of Christ. I gave them a
tortoise and the Annunciation. I gave them a woman
having a drink in a pub. And a woman lounging in her
bath. I gave them naked women reposing beneath the
lilacs. And the girl in a mask."

"And what did they give you, Love?"

"A burial."

LEVON: "Vehicle transmitting dead ahead. Anticipate
encounter. Block Loma Vista. Repeat—block Loma
Vista . . ."

"What do you mean, a *burial*?"

"Well, they all buried me a little. They embalmed
me. Isn't that what they do? The youth and beauty

and talent, all of it's sucked out and offered to the incense burners. Now don't you worry, we take care of everything—oh, we have stock coffins, and we'll just fill your abdominal cavities with a mixture of sawdust and sand. We'll put your intestines in canopic jars. And would you like two rams to guard your house, your *residence*? Perhaps two black jackals, or a gazelle? And you just feed us with your images and we'll suck them out of you until you're dessicated. And when I, the great nebula star, croak, there will be a place for you in the pyramid. You'll be in the side room with the mummified ducks and the embalmed shrew mouse, and the pertrified scarab beetles. We will all be preserved, perfect in golden celluloid."

LEVON: "Vehicle leaving road. Suspect vehicle using fire road from Franklin Canyon. Repeat—vehicle using fire road. Believe he's seen us . . . he's seen us . . ."

Lichteiman heard the crying, the weeping.

"Love, what's wrong?"

"They've taken my guts."

"I'm sorry, Love. Where are you, Love? Let me come meet you, and help you, Love . . ."

"*Home*. I'm almost home."

"Wait, Love . . ."

The transmission ended.

4:27 A.M.

Marjorie decided to turn on Roxbury and cross over to Lexington to hit Coldwater. As she came up the hill, she heard the first of the sirens. A cop car raced past her at a tremendous speed, followed by a second. It didn't have any particular meaning to her. It wasn't an unusual sight, help dashing for a canyon crash or fire. It could have even been a burglary in Laurel Hills. By the time she reached Valley Road she could see the gaggle of flashing lights and police cars. She decided it had to be a wreck; there were so many car accidents at that bend, and she just hoped no one had been hurt. The worst wreck she had ever seen at that point was a Lincoln limousine which smashed into a Ferrari; miraculously everyone walked away.

4:31 A.M.

Lichteiman finished checking the surveillance data himself, and even though Levon reported the transmission halted at a point where a car could emerge from a fire road anywhere from Mulholland as far down as Cherokee, he felt the data indicated Love lived closer to the top of the canyon. The transmission showed Love's car had been ascending on Coldwater when the transmission broke, on the words *"Home. I'm almost home."* Lichteiman also felt quite certain that Love supposed they were homing in on the transmission in one way or another. At this point, Lichteiman knew the killer was in his greatest darkness, begging from his soul to be caught before he reached the ones he loved.

"To Rover Four, cover Loma Vista to Cherokee light." Lichteiman began to choreograph the police cars via his car radio.

"To Rover Two start below Cherokee, cover east and west side streets."

"To Rover Five, Coldwater from Heather to Eden."

All cars cut in, to answer, acknowledged instructions received. They were beating the bushes, but so far no signs of strange cruising or of a parked car with unusual broadcast antenna.

"To all Rovers—exercise extreme caution. *Extreme* caution . . ."

Lichteiman decided he himself would start at the top of Coldwater at a point where a huge new home was being constructed on a landfill just below the canyon crest. Coming down slowly on the left was a tremendous rise leading to a water tower. On the right were driveways, one leading to Charlton Heston's home, and several other celebrity properties. The first street off Coldwater to the left was Deep Canyon Place. He checked it, saw nothing suspicious. No cars, in driveways or on the street, remotely equipped as Love's must be. Back on Coldwater, he remembered the Tree People Road and a small park. From those he came back on down to Loonridge. He was about to drive into its cul de sac when a radio message came in.

"To Lichteiman, Rover Five in need of assistance. Urgent. 1080 urgent. We have a 1080 urgent at Coldwater near Valley . . ."

4:32 A.M.

When Marjorie reached the top of the canyon, she turned and started down into Valley Road. She noticed the wall and gate lights were on at the Stark's house. They must have heard the crash, Marjorie decided. Even though Melissa and her husband had one of the homes with the largest piece of property on Valley Road, Marjorie thought the traffic, no less the accidents, on Coldwater must drive them insane. Marjorie had played tennis on Melissa's court once and the noise was so distracting she could hardly keep track of her game.

Just past the first turn her headlights caught a figure at the gates. It was Melissa in a white robe, talking to one of her maids. Marjorie pulled the Volvo over, and ran up the driveway.

"Melissa, what's going on?"

"I think someone was killed," Melissa said, belting her robe tighter around her waist. "Somebody said it was some blond woman with a Mercedes—I sent the houseboy up to check it out."

"Oh, God . . ."

"You look like you're going to pass out, Marjorie."

"Melissa, could I call my house?"

"Of course." Melissa held Marjorie's arm as they scrambled up the rest of the driveway to the house. The maid took her other arm until they reached the porch that surrounded the sprawling home. Marjorie didn't want to make the connection, but she felt it. She felt it and it was making her weak and dazed. Her mind fought it, and if she hadn't been so disoriented, she would have noticed the Seville turning off Coldwater and rolling down Valley Road—the Seville slowing as it went by her white Volvo on the street. Instead, she used all her sanity and strength to get in the front door and wade through the decorated hallway to the phone. She dialed her home and it rang; *and it rang.* She let it ring a full five minutes before hanging up.

4:41 A.M.

Lichteiman did not have to stay at the murder site for the coroner's full report. He could see the ripping, the nail marks about the neck and breasts. The head was found thirty feet from the body. He knew, from the very few other cases of decapitation by human hands he had ever heard of, that only the adrenaline-charged strength of complete madness could accomplish such a feat. He stayed no longer than ten minutes before getting back to his car. "All Rover units tighten to final circle. Repeat. Final circle . . ."

Lichteiman himself drove back to the vantage point of Loonridge. With the murder so near by, he would have to check each home, each cul de sac.

The blackness of Franklin Canyon lay out beyond the seven or eight homes of the existing development. He knew immediately that Love did not live on this street. No eucalyptus trees. Only a few small pines leading down to a metal barrier shining far down at the end of the street. He was about to turn around when his lights caught the reflectors of a car parked to the right of the barrier next to the rim of an arroyo. A car with a telephone antenna.

Lichteiman parked his car, began to walk along the pitted rock and sandy covering of the dead-end street. Even from where he stood he knew it was a Seville, from the lines of the two-tone paint job: two shades of tan with a hatchback effect. He slowed as he closed in on the car. Then, when he was certain it was empty, he began to absorb its every detail. California license plate 1AOF599, spoke wheels, most ripped from curb parking. Windows open. Good rubber treads. Twisted hood crest ornament: one olive leaf broken. Inside, mounted below dashboard, was a standard car phone, along with special equipment for broadcast, reception, radio. Special tape deck: play, record, standard cassette plus microcassette attachments. Custom power antenna, no phone number marked. No special transmission bands or operator license numbers.

He opened the driver's door, began to check under the seats, the floor mats. Candy wrappers. Pieces of orange candy in ashtrays. Piece of gold cord left from gift wrapping. McDonald's contest form. Glove compartment: Seville owner's manual, "Success Motivation" cassette, other tapes—"He's Your Dog, Charlie Brown," Barry Manilow's "One Voice."

Lichteiman went back to his car.

"Rover Two. Rover Two. Lichteiman to Rover Two."

"We hear you."

"Suspect's vehicle at Loonridge. I'm going out Ridge Path. Will maintain contact while in area."

"You got it."

Lichteiman attached his transmitter to his belt before opening the trunk of his car. Love could be on the ridge path waiting for him, but he didn't think it likely. He also doubted Love was fleeing into the jungle bush of the far canyon. More likely, Lichteiman believed, Love was doing what he said he was going to do. *Love was going home.*

Lichteiman took his high-powered telescopic rifle, and began to walk out beyond the cul de sac along the fire-access path. As he walked he could see that the ridge ran along just above the larger, more settled community of Lost Orchard. He looked down on the collection of large homes nestling below in their lush walled and landscaped settings. From this height it looked like a doll-house village, but the most arresting sight for Lichteiman was the great eucalyptus grove that ran the length of the valley.

4:45 A.M.

Marjorie remained on a large white wicker bench in Melissa Stark's hallway. She had called her own house a second time, and still there was no answer. Melissa had gone off to wake up her maid and start coffee, and the house boy had gone back up to the scene of the *accident.*

Carole had said she was going to call Maria and get her over to the house, Marjorie remembered. Perhaps Maria's car wasn't working and Carole had gone to pick her up. Sometimes Maria had her boyfriend bring her, but maybe he wasn't around with his truck, perhaps he'd gone fishing or down to Mexico for the weekend. Sometimes he took his truck and loaded it up with cheap tile in Tijuana and sold it at a huge profit in Beverly Hills. But Carole had seemed so drunk; and the big fire in the den fireplace!

Marjorie had to close her eyes against the whiteness of Melissa's hallway. *Perfectly fine wood flooring painted white, clocks, vases, jardinieres, Palos Verdes rocks—all painted white!* She sat in limbo, breathing denials. She didn't like all the information flowing through her; her brain ticked, echoed. The possibilities ricocheted inside her skull, setting off brief sparks of understanding. It was coming together in spite of what she wished. She burst into tears. In a moment Melissa was at her side, holding onto her.

"I've got to talk to someone. Jesus Christ, I've got to talk . . ."

She began to pour it out. Not the *milk,* she couldn't tell Melissa about the milk, or what he had done with Courtney. She didn't even want to tell her about the cocaine. Instead, through great sobs she blurted out as much of her pain as she could bear.

"How can I live, Melissa, oh God, how can I live without affection, he hasn't been giving me warmth, there's been no warmth for so long, when I'm sitting close to him on the sofa he moves away, he always moves away, he wants distance from me . . . he turns to ice . . . when I go to him and put my arms around him he turns to ice . . . I touch him and I feel like I'm sitting next to a stranger and here we are in the same room, my husband and I in the same room and *he's* . . ."

"I'm sorry, Marjorie . . I'm so sorry . . ."

". . . the only time he holds me is when he's *fucking* me . . . oh, God, and once in a while, walking he'll take my hand . . . but there's been no affection for so long, and there's no physical warmth and I don't know what to do. I don't know what to do. He's sick, he's very sick and I can't, I can't . . . he doesn't really know me or my body, my husband doesn't really know who I am, and I don't know who he is and I don't know how to handle it . . . I just sat there and let it build up and I've been in such pain . . . I'm so sorry, Melissa, so sorry to be pouring this on you . . ."

"It's okay," Melissa comforted, hugging her tighter, caring. "Just get it out."

"He's what he is," Marjorie cried, "he's constantly thinking. I've talked to him a lot, he knows his shortcomings, he's just not affectionate. It's not in him. I've tried to tell him what I need, I need to be kissed, I need to be touched. He knows I reach out to him and he turns to stone. We've talked about it. It's not like it's a mystery, and yet he can't do anything about it . . . and he's gotten very, very sick . . ."

"What do you mean *sick*?"

"He's depressed, he's in trouble . . . Oh, God, we've been going broke, he's been under terrible pressure . . . and maybe it's partly my fault, my fault because I don't know about money, I never was taught how to be a wife . . ."

"You've been a good wife . . ."

"I just feel I've been avoiding something, there's something I need to face . . ."

"You can't face it all at once," Melissa said soothingly.

"I don't think it's wrong for me to want to be loved . . . *Loved* . . ." The word caught in her throat, drew out into a plea. "*Love . . . I'm not wrong, it's not my fault I have needs and I don't want to talk about the kids, it's just him and me, it's just him and me! And I don't know what to do, I don't know how to help him or help myself I'm so confused.* I don't know what to do. He's so sick and I do feel sorry for him . . . I don't think he knows who he is . . . he's hidden from himself and everyone else . . . and it's making him diseased and killing him. I know there is something *dying*, something is eating him alive without him knowing, he doesn't know . . . he doesn't know . . ."

5:00 A.M.

And then, the terrible ringing. Melissa answered the phone.

"It's for you, Marjorie," Melissa said. "Do you feel . . . able to take it. Are you *okay?*"

"Who is it?" Marjorie asked, her voice was too thin, weak. *Who could it be since no one knows I'm here? The Volvo. Someone must have seen the Volvo.*

She took the receiver as Melissa moved discreetly back toward the kitchen.

"*Hello.*"

A silence, but the line was open. She knew someone was listening. Someone was there.

Finally a voice, "*Hello, Marjorie?*"

She recognized his voice. It was lower, exhausted—chilling.

"What do you want, Jack?" She knew her voice was cracking, that she wouldn't be able to hold back the scream much longer.

"Come *home*," the voice said. "I've got the children, Marjorie. *I've got the children . . .*"

Marjorie couldn't speak. She heard a fumbling with the phone. The phone was being passed.

"Mommy, please come home, mommy!"

It was her Courtney. "Oh my God! Oh my God!" Marjorie was shouting now. The phone sounds. It was being passed again. Mumblings of her children at a distance. "Courtney, where are you?" Marjorie cried.

Then only his low voice: "Come home, Marjorie," he said, his voice crawling, barely moving. "Come home. *I want us all to be buried together.*"

Click. He hung up.

Marjorie was screaming. She tried to dial. The phone fell from her hands. Melissa rushed in from the kitchen. Others. The maid.

"Get the police," Marjorie begged, running down the whiteness of the hall, yanking open the front door. *"My husband has my kids! He wants to kill my kids! All of us!"* She screamed, lurching onto the porch. "The police. Get the police . . ." She was stumbling now. "Help me! Oh, God! Help me!" she shrieked behind her.

Marjorie rattled down the steps to the driveway, then headed down the incline to the street. The gate was closed. Melissa had closed her huge white gate with the sharp pointed spears; Marjorie was locked in. "Open the gate! Oh God! Open the gate! For Christ's sake, let me out!" she screamed at the top of her lungs, pulling and kicking at the white bars. Somewhere the switch was thrown. The motor started and the gate jerked and slid open, nearly trapping Marjorie's hand between the gratings. She was out on the street now, running down the hill past the Volvo. It would be faster without the car, she decided. And help. She'd get help. She ran past other gates and walls. "Help, oh, please help me . . ." The only home

without a gate had such a sharp climb up the driveway she would never make it. She veered to the yellow
line at the center of the road. She would scream as she
ran.

"Please!" she cried. "Please somebody help me!"

She ran past the great mounds of ivy; a rat scurried from one hiding place to another, and she could
hear the movements of other small animals from
deeper within. The next house on the left was Roger
Mercer's; the gate was closed, a blue-and-white security sign slapped into her face. She couldn't find the
buzzer, the doorbell, just a tremendously ornate mailbox with brass ponies pulling a surrey. On the right
was Gene Frankel's house. She began pressing the
black wrought-iron arm that reached out in front of
his gate, but a tremendous growling and gnashing of
teeth began—his Dobermans, wanting to tear her to
pieces. She ran, tripping in the potholes and cracks
from flood erosions. Now there was a high chain-link
fence on both sides of her, sealing off the estates, tremendous rolls of barbed wire lurking beneath the
flower vines and bougainvillea. She ran past the tennis courts, the servants' cars. At one point a coyote
stood in a driveway simply watching her. Long before
she had reached the bottom of the hill she realized no
help would be coming. She could barely think. She
came around the corner of the plastic surgeon's lot,
his tennis court, and saw her house.

She wouldn't be able to find her keys. The Genie.
She'd press the hidden Genie button to the right of
the garage.

The dogs! Why isn't Sam barking? Sandy?

An initial scrape and growl, and then the hum of
the motor, lifting, cranking the huge black door of the
garage up into the darkness of the ceiling. There was

no time for planning. For intelligence. She had to do what her instincts told her. "Courtney! Danny!" she shrieked.

Why aren't the dogs barking?

She headed into the garage, past the discarded bureaus and electric lawn mower and leaf blower. Her eyes drank in everything—the yellow labels on the Olympic paint cans; the snail and slug poisons. The can of gasoline. She found herself instinctively searching for *weapons*.

Suddenly, the automatic motor kicked in and the garage door began its descent behind her. She saw a form, something attached to the door. At first it was a shadow, coming down from the blackness of the ceiling. As she turned she saw the inverted body.

It was nailed upside-down on the descending garage door. Before the light from the Genie cut out she was able to see sneakers, white socks, brown skin, the long black hair hanging down. What she had subliminally perceived as an oil slick on the floor was not oil at all, but drippings from the crucified corpse of Maria.

CHAPTER SEVENTEEN

5:05 A.M.

Lichteiman sat on the Sandy canyon ground, leaning his back against the thick trunk of a pine tree on the ridge. He wondered what Love would look like, what his face would be. Would he be grateful? Disappointed? Dead? And if he was taken alive, what would Love think of this fat, messy detective in the soiled safari jacket—this wreck of a telephone confidant, receiver of bloody ovaries? And what if he, Lichteiman, had read the writings of Love? What if he had been able to read something which had been written from Love's deepest purity. Now he looked out past the canyons, his rifle across his lap—out through slivers of distant fog. He let his mind lift high once more, flying out of his body in a waiting nightdream. He made Love appear in his brain, and he began to speak to him—*What will you do, Love? Kill them all . . . ?*

The children shrieking in the distance.

Marjorie spun from the dangling, mutilated body of Maria.

Her son and daughter alive! She opened the door and came into the servants' stairwell. She didn't care if Jack was waiting for her. She didn't care if he was behind a door or near the ovens as she moved fast, *faster*. She began to run the length of the house, past the den and sunroom, and the still-burning fire. Past the center hall and the gaping living room.

The dogs. Where are the dogs?

Danny was still calling for her, crying. And when she reached the edge of the library Marjorie saw him at the far end of the room. Her little son sitting stiff, erect, helpless in the Eames chair, reaching out for her, Courtney at his side.

"Mommy! Mommy!"

Except for her children, the library was empty. No one behind the desk. No one lurking beneath the imported marble and Italian leather. Nothing between Marjorie and her living children. She ran to them, and now their arms were around her. She lifted them up, kissing them, their skin chilled with fear. She checked their arms and limbs and throats. There were no marks; just her Courtney and Danny alive.

"He made us stay here. He said we couldn't get out of the chair, Mommy," Danny cried.

"Where is he, Danny?" Marjorie asked, barely moving her lips.

Courtney was shaking, pointing beyond the vast glass wall to the garden outside.

Marjorie took a few steps, her arms molding her children to her chest. Then she put them down, held their hands. She would move slowly, she decided. She'd keep her eyes on the carpet, the wine-colored carpet, and begin to walk back out of the library. She knew he was watching her from the garden. Watching mother and children behind the glass of the doors. Finally, she saw him standing at the edge of the stone trim of the rose garden and shadows of the eucalyptus trees. He was naked. Waiting. She would move slowly with her son and daughter. If she went too swiftly she knew she would trigger an animal instinct in him, that he would rush forward, reach her before she could get out. If her motions were correct, she believed—if they were humble enough, Madonna and children, perhaps the thing in the garden would let them go. And the *dogs*. She saw them now, lifeless dark forms floating in the pool—and realized why they weren't barking. The rabbit cage glistened from the depths of the deep end.

"Where's the bunnies, Mommy?"

"Later, honey, we'll talk about it later . . ."

Marjorie felt a pain rip across her chest. She would have to keep the paralyzing horror away for just a few more moments. She started to panic, to increase her speed. And she made the mistake of looking toward the garden.

He was running now, running at her.

She got to the end of the living room before the crash. Her husband had hurtled his entire body through the wall of glass, and he was falling upon her. She screamed above the explosion, and his naked body just missed her and the kids.

Now she was rushing up the center hallway, the spiral stairs, nearly lifting Courtney and Danny off the ground. She was at the front door with the three locks. Hands trembling, she threw the top bolt.

The middle lock jammed. Marjorie let out a cry of frustration.

She could hear the animal coming up the stairs after her. She fled from the doors, up the few steps to the second landing. Now she was in Courtney's room, closing the door, wedging a chair under the door knob. Courtney was crying, and Marjorie motioned her onto the bed. Danny stood alert, ready. With one motion she knocked the dolls off Courtney's workbench. Grabbing the bench, she jammed it against the door as the animal began to hurl into it from the other side. The room shook.

But somehow, the door was holding.

She ran to the window, slid half of it to the left. A three-foot railing of wrought iron was her only obstacle. She would have to climb up onto the railing and leap out—but the ground fell away too quickly down to a cement moat. Her children's heads might crack open. She could land on her feet, but her legs might break. Even if they survived the leap, they might be trapped down there. She began to scream across to the flickering light in the home across the street. Dr. Huston—the plastic surgeon—he was home! He was watching television! He would hear their screaming.

5:15 A.M.

Lichteiman heard the crash from up on the ridge. He knew it was glass. It *could* have been a car crash, someone slowing to look at the accident scene over on Coldwater. The canyons played tricks with echoes. But this was different. And now screaming. A woman screaming.

One of the houses below seemed rather brightly lit for this time of night. The stream of multicolored garden lights and floodlamps in the other lush backyards dimmed compared to the long, white two-story home—where the eucalyptus grove between the house and ridge was particularly thick. Lichteiman walked farther along the ridge, straining for a better view, giving the final orders.

"All Rovers to Valley Road at Lost Orchard . . . Valley Road, Lost Orchard . . ."

"To all special operations: heavy cars urgently required. Three men with vests, three snipers completely equipped."

"To communications, all-area alert. Extreme caution. Dangerous and unpredictable, wanted for multiple homicides."

The woman still screaming.

"To assault homicide, second repeat. Emergency assistance at Valley Road, Lost Orchard."

Lichteiman paused, both hands on his rifle now. The old rulebook of his brain told him to hurry back to his car, drive down from the ridge onto Coldwater and circle on to the valley—but his instinct told him to remain on the high ground. Somewhere in the glowing hamlet below, he knew Love was having his finale.

5:17 A.M.

Marjorie felt the warm blast of porch lights flood the front of the surgeon's home. Through her screams and tears she saw the front door open and the doctor looking at her. For a moment she was afraid he would turn and run back in. But no, he was running down the steps, coming out his front gate, rushing for the street and her home.

"He's trying to kill us! *He wants to kill us!*" she screamed at the puzzled, worried face.

Suddenly, the pounding on the door to Courtney's room stopped, and Marjorie rushed to the door to listen. She could hear the thumping of the animal leaping down the steps. He was fumbling through something. Metal sounds. Hollow brass. He was getting something from the umbrella stand, from the hat rack. She heard him working the locks free as the surgeon pressed the doorbell, banged on the door.

She rushed back to the window screaming, "Get away! Get away! Don't, doctor, don't . . ."

Her warnings were lost in the toyroom, smothered among the heaps of lace-gowned dolls. She sprang to the window. She leaned out, still screaming, *warning*. She saw the surgeon and he was looking at her. She heard the noise—the front door being opened swiftly. Before the surgeon could understand or look away from her eyes, she saw the pair of hands emerge into her view. They held a closed umbrella, its long, pointed metal tip protruding from the folded overlays of black, shiny cloth. But it was happening too fast to stop.

The staff crashed forward, piercing the doctor's chest. The doctor cried out, a dry cracking of bone and a great rush of deep crushed breath—and then fell.

Marjorie heard the front door slam shut, locks clicking back into place.

"The tree house, Mommy," Danny said firmly.

The tree house.

She grabbed Danny and Courtney, kicked the chair and workbench aside. She opened the door. Now they were out running past Danny's room and down the steps to the kitchen. There wouldn't be time to go out through the garage. She could hear the animal after them again. She raced into the sunroom, pulled at a slab of glass, and it slid open. She ran past the pool, with its dark shadows of floating dead animals, out across the back lawn and beyond to the rose garden and eucalyptus trees. Her mind drank in the entire yard, considering each and every object: the bird feeder, the azaleas, the pool; the rose thorns, the patio furniture; the hose, *the tree house*.

"Up, Danny up! Up, Courtney."

Danny climbed as fast as a monkey, pulling Courtney up along with him. They would be safe. If the thing came after them, they could climb higher, higher.

"Come, Mommy! Come on, Mommy!" Danny cried down to her.

"Hurry, Mommy!"

"No. *Just stay there. Stay up there!*"

Danny started to come down.

"I said stay up there!"

She turned, looked back toward the house. For a moment it seemed the animal was gone. It was only her naked husband walking slowly, sadly, toward them. He was carrying a plastic bag filled with whiteness. It looked like a gift. Something for her.

She ran further to the darkest part of the grounds, near the tennis court. She was gauging the distance carefully. If he went after the children first, she would have to *stop* him.

Jack followed her, then stopped, peering uncertainly into the deep gloom of the shrubbery. Marjorie saw him hesitate, then she felt her legs grow heavy as he moved away, closer to the tree which held the playhouse. He stopped. She wouldn't, *couldn't* do anything yet—the children were high in the great tree's branches, and she felt even if he tried to climb up the thin wooden slats nailed into the tree would never support his weight. She would wait in the shadows. He wouldn't hurt the children. He had scared them, but never really *hurt* them.

"Danny," she heard him call up into the labyrinth of branches and vines. His voice was low, calm.

"Don't come up, Daddy," Danny called down.

"I *have* to Danny . . ."

"No, Daddy," Courtney said.

Marjorie strained to see. The thick ivy and clustered eucalyptus trees formed a maze of black and silver leaves, tangled further by giant twisted shavings of hanging bark. She moved slowly to one side, glimpsed Jack placing the plastic bag up into a gnarl of branches. Then he began to climb.

5:20 A.M.

Danny and Courtney looked down from the small door of their tree house. They could see their father starting up toward them, the wooden slats creaking, splitting. They saw him slip, begin to fall, but his strong hands reached out like an ape's and gripped the tree's branches to stop his descent. From below they heard their mother screaming up to them.

"DON'T LET HIM TOUCH YOU! DON'T LET HIM NEAR YOU!"

"Don't come up, Daddy!" Danny shouted down again. "Don't. Please, don't!"

Again, their mother's voice reached them through the darkness. "DON'T TOUCH THEM, JACK! DON'T TOUCH THEM! OH, GOD, GOD . . ."

Courtney began to cry, to move anxiously back and forth in the small house. Its thin, weathered cedar planks squeaked and groaned even under her slight weight.

"HE'S NOT YOUR FATHER! HE'S NOT YOUR FATHER NOW! HE'S AN ANIMAL! YOU KNOW THAT, DANNY, DON'T YOU?"

"He's Daddy," Courtney cried, "He's *Daddy* . . ."

They heard a crash below, and their mother cried out. The children sensed she had only tripped, stumbled. Their ears were picking up every sound now. They could separate the movements of their mother circling the brush near the tennis court from those of the grunting, naked father-animal now moving steadily toward them.

Danny leaned out of the doorway of the playhouse. His father would reach them in a moment. He saw his sister weeping now, sitting in a corner near one of the tiny windows. His mother was screaming up to them again, trying to tell them what to do.

"Don't come any further," Danny warned his father. He could see his father's eyes now, see his chest heaving with great intakes of air while his legs clung to the bark, his feet gripping the trunk like a telephone repairman going up a pole. Danny saw his father staring back at him, saw the look in his eyes. His mother was right. He mustn't touch them, mustn't catch them!

"It's a witch," Danny shouted at Courtney as he turned back into the playhouse. "It's a witch that looks like Daddy!" He ran to a toy stove they had dragged up for a make-believe Thanksgiving dinner in November. He opened the little oven and reached inside for his special mud balls. He grabbed two in his hands and rushed back to the door. "Help me stop the witch!" he screamed at Court, as he began to throw the mud balls down at the beast. "Help me!" he yelled again, running back and forth, hurling his meager weapons downward. Courtney stopped crying, managed to stand knowing she would have to help.

"DON'T HURT THEM, JACK! OH, GOD, DON'T HURT THEM!"

Courtney began passing the mud balls to Danny. She knew he had hidden rocks inside some of them. When she handed him the last of them, she stood next to her brother and looked down to see if the *witch* had been stopped. It was still coming, a little more slowly, brushing dirt from its eyes. But the witch's hands now had hold of the branches which held the tree house, and the house began to shake. Hairy fingers gripped the bottom of the doorway as Danny ran to the oven again, moved it aside to reveal a very large mud ball, his "super" weapon. He grasped it in both arms and headed for the doorway as Courtney grabbed her tea tray. They reached the doorway together. Courtney flung the pot and cups and saucers down on the witch, his face now twisted with rage. The hand of the witch shot in, grabbed her ankle and she screamed as it began to drag her out the door.

"No!" Danny yelled, dropping the mud-rock onto the invader, kicking at its arm until it let his sister free again. He rushed Courtney to the rear window and the two of them climbed out as the beast pulled itself inside the treehouse.

5:22 A.M.

Lichteiman slid down the steep bank of the canyon, closer and closer to the screams. He was stopped dead by a high link fence encrusted with vines and had to fight to find a clearing in the green webbing through which to see further below. He heard the woman screaming. She seemed closer somehow, but there were cries from somewhere up above. Children. *Children.* Something was frightening children in a tree.

By the time he had positioned his rifle and peered through its infra-red scope, all he could see were two children high in a giant tree—as far out on a limb as they could go. A larger form was moving toward them, something primitive like a stalking naked ape. He wanted to call out to Love, but he was so far away. He knew he would have to shoot him before he reached the children, but the branches and great cascades of vines obscured Love, gave him cover. Instinct made him point the rifle straight up into the sky and fire. Perhaps it would warn the beast, sober it.

5:24 A.M.

Marjorie, still scratched and bleeding from her fall, spun with surprise and hope at the sound of the rifle shot. It seemed to come from the canyon side, from near the distant fence or even one of the houses as far up as Loonridge. But then she heard the voice, booming from *too* far away.

"It's YOU he wants! It's YOU he wants!"

She turned toward the anonymous voice. Some-one was up on the ridge, someone watching them, someone shouting to her.

She fell again in confusion and fear.

She needed light.

She pulled herself along the tennis court fence, flinging her hands one after the other—letting her fingers sink into the mesh to guide her, support her. Finally she was through the single-gated entrance, and knew with certain dread she was entering a cage. She ran to the far corner and threw the switch—pray-ing the circuit breaker wouldn't kick out as it some-times did. At first the dozen huge lanterns only sparked and flickered. Then, finally, the flicker grew into powerful fingers of light.

"I'M *HERE*, JACK!" she screamed up into the tree. She was frozen by the sight of Danny and Courtney dangerously far from the thick trunk, cling-ing to one of the slender clusters of branches and vines in the huge tree. Then, to her relief, she saw Jack's attention moving from the children to her, watched him back away to the juncture of the tree house and slowly lower himself to the ground. He reached back up into the branches. In a moment he had the plastic bag of white powder again, and was moving toward her. Her relief was transformed into a new and immediate terror.

"Don't hurt Mommy, Daddy! Don't hurt Mommy!"

Her mind continued to concentrate on her surroundings: the automatic server, the net, the wrench. A few sad tennis balls sat like yellow eyes staring from dark corners.

He came into the tennis cage with her. She moved to put the net between them.

"Please don't hurt Mommy! Don't hurt Mommy, Daddy. Don't hurt her!" the children cried.

"I'm all right," Marjorie called back to the kids—but she knew she wasn't.

"It won't hurt, Marjorie," Jack promised, beginning to open the plastic bag. He looked otherworldly under the assault of lights, his messed, wild black hair and night eyes in striking contrast with his white skin. He stood before her. In a moment he was weeping. It froze her heart when she realized that he was looking at her with tenderness.

"I love you, Marjorie, but I *have* to."

"Jack . . ."

She could hear the police sirens in the distance. They were coming. But they would get lost. They always got lost on Valley Road. The two streets had duplicate numbers. What had happened to the man with the gun? She started screaming again for help.

Jack moved to the end of the net and pressed the release. The net floated down between them, and she fell silent. Now that there was nothing between them, her screaming seemed rather ridiculous. She looked at him. She decided to try speaking sensibly. *Please don't kill me. I'll be entertaining. I'll let you hold me, and do anything you want to me, and I'll cook and kiss . . . and whatever you do don't hurt me . . . don't hurt me and our children . . .*

Suddenly her body stopped shaking. She couldn't speak. She found there were no more words for her and to her own shock, she found herself running *at* him. She felt herself punching and clawing him.

She tore the white plastic bag from Jack's hands, but his arms slowly closed around her in an embrace. His arms tightened, and tightened. He was forcing her down now, pulling her down onto the court. She tried to pull her arms free, but he was too strong. She brought both her fists up and pushed them into his face. Then she was wedged between his legs and he brought her arms behind her. Finally, with one free hand he reached into the bag and brought out a handful of the whiteness and tried to force it into her mouth.

"Don't hurt Mommy!"

The sirens wailed closer.

"Help! Oh God! Help!" She cried out as his fingers pushed their way into her mouth. The white choking powder burning, numbing . . .

"It will be like a dream," he promised.

"It will be like a dream, I love you I love you."

She was so weak. He was completely over her now with more of the whiteness, literally pushing it down her throat.

"No, Daddy! No!"

"Help me! Somebody help!"

Then when he knew he was in control, he relaxed and stood above her. He lifted her head to his groin and continued to feed her . . . to feed her the whiteness. She felt one of his tears fall onto her face, and then he stopped. He touched her with a great tenderness.

"I see you, Marjorie," he said. *"Do you see me?"*

She lowered her hands from above, from all protection.

"I see you," she said. "I see you now, Jack . . ."
"Love. It's over!"
Marjorie heard the husky, commanding voice. She looked across the court and saw the fat old man in his torn safari jacket holding a rifle.

Lichteiman moved slowly forward under the glare of lights, relaxed, his rifle held loosely at his side. Half his concentration was directed at the woman: *Move away, lady, move away from him . . .*
Love turned, looked straight at him.
Hold his stare. Hold him, Lichteiman told himself.
Lichteiman smiled gently, hiding the shock he felt at the sight before him, at the sickening evidence of the complete degradation of a human being. Lichteiman wanted him to know: *I understand your fear and desire to hurt. I understand your need . . .* He tried to communicate these thoughts with his eyes, quickly. There would be no more than an instant. He could already hear the sounds of other men as Love moved forward, arms extended. Then, from beyond the darkness, came the shots, echoing like cracks of thunder.

Marjorie saw her husband's body lift, blown back as though by some heavy object, before her mind recognized the rifle shots. Under the hot white light of the tennis court Jack's body collapsed.
She stayed still, not believing. Then she ran to his body, saw his shattered skull, the fragments of bone and brains and blood. Then she was leaving him, the chain-link of the tennis court blurring as she raced for her children. Danny jumped down from the lowest rung of the tree.
Danny and Courtney safe. Alive.

She ran with them back past the pool, heard the other police cars screeching to a halt in front of the house. The front doorbell was ringing, chiming, *banging*.

Marjorie raced with the children into the sunroom and up the stairs to the front door.

She heard the sounds of men moving, rushing, shouting.

They were calling for her. In the darkness she let go of her children's hands and began to slide the bolts, turn the locks. In a moment the door would open to the crowd of reassuring, blue-uniformed policemen. She would look beyond them to the distant horizon, to the first signs that soon dawn would be there.